THE MASTER OF PEN Y BRYN

THE MASTER OF PEN Y BRYN

A story from the period of the Tithe War

E TEGLA DAVIES

Translated from the Welsh by Nina Watkins

CHRISTOPHER DAVIES

First Published 1975

Published by
Christopher Davies (Publishers) Ltd
Llandybie
Dyfed

Printed by
Salesbury Press Ltd
Llandybie
Dyfed

ISBN 07154 0179 3

Published with the support of
The Welsh Arts Council

Chapter I

The Master of Pen y Bryn (or so he told his wife, Jane) felt that he was getting old and decrepit, and for that reason, he said, the farm and the responsibility it involved were too much for him: and she agreed. He decided to call on David Hughes the carpenter on his way to the prayer meeting, and to ask him to come home with him that evening for a chat and to offer a word of advice. Not that he felt in need of advice, for he was a man with a very high opinion of his own counsel; in other words, the type of man who likes asking all manner of people for advice, the answer being implicit in the question the whole time. Once he has received the answer he had already given himself, he indulges in a bout of private self-congratulation, thinking himself as shrewd as the whole neighbourhood put together. So whose advice should he ask first but that of David Hughes? For everyone was likely to agree with *him*, and David Hughes would probably agree with the Master of Pen y Bryn, particularly if it was to his advantage to do so.

David Hughes, the carpenter, was general adviser to the neighbourhood, and his word was law. He welcomed this opportunity to be indispensable, and was as ready with his advice as people were to ask for it. The moment the fellowship meeting was over, the two of them set off at a half-trot across the fields towards Pen y Bryn; and the congregation stood in the road watching them. Everyone had noticed that there was something up; the Master of Pen y Bryn had opened the service by announcing some pretty short hymns; he had read a short psalm; and his prayers had been brief — and he was very long-winded, as a rule. And David Hughes had refused to say one word at the meeting. Anyway, off they went, ignoring everybody; the Master of Pen y Bryn was too preoccupied with his advancing years to remember his decrepitude even, and David Hughes was too wrapped in his private secrets and his own counsel to notice anything. Little Shôn, one of the farm labourers at Pen y Bryn, followed about ten yards behind like a faithful dog. Shôn had to follow his master to chapel and back whenever the latter found it convenient to go, because his master felt that a bit of guidance was important at his age. Shôn, to brighten his solitude, amused himself by giving a subjective portrait of his leaders to all the passers-by — that is, when he felt that there was some empathy between himself and his audience. Shôn's method of portraiture was to raise the index finger of his left hand and the closed fist of his right. The figure one represented the Master of Pen y Bryn; the 'o' was David Hughes. This was as good a representation of them as could be desired; for the Master of Pen y Bryn was a tall, thin man, with a wrinkled face and an anxious expression. Shôn's way of depicting this anxiety was to bend the tip of his finger slightly towards the ground. The carpenter was about the same height as the Master of Pen y Bryn, but he ovoid, without a wrinkle or a stoop; like an egg, too, he bulged out in the middle and got thinner at top and bottom. After that evening, when people talked about Number Ten everyone knew what they meant. David Hughes' part of the numeral was not, it is true, particularly flattering, since it implied that he was a nobody apart from the Master of Pen y Bryn. David Hughes' good fortune in life inspired in him a desire to offer advice, and a desire to solicit it in other people; and altogether it was pretty good advice, even far-sighted as well.

The two men slowed their pace — they had to, since David Hughes was one of them — and embarked on a deep discussion about all manner of things. The Master of Pen y Bryn kept trying to find a suitable peg on which he could hang his tale, and the carpenter, in his own quiet way, gave him every assistance by smiling away pleasantly like summer sunshine, which was unusual for him. The Master of Pen y Bryn was absolutely right about the weather, the carpenter said with emphasis, but although they were in complete agreement on this point the peg did not begin to appear, and the Master of Pen y Bryn postponed his efforts till a more favourable moment should arise. It was amusing to follow them, as Shôn was doing, from a distance of ten yards or so. Their voices mingled — you could not discern the words — with an effect rather like the two sounds made by a mill. The Master of Pen y Bryn made a nervous, whispering noise, the voiceless, incessant sigh of the water rushing over the wheel; David Hughes made the low grinding sound. Shôn told Robin Y Ddôl this once, forgetting that David Hughes was his uncle. Robin replied that a mill produced three kinds of noise, and that the third was made by the creature who acted as beast of burden. Shôn did not find this completed description very flattering to himself — after all, he was one of the trio that night — so he was effectively silenced.

It was a peaceful, pleasant, magical night towards the end of September; the sky was clearer and the stars brighter than at any other time of year. The landscape was illuminated by a harvest moon. No wonder our elders used to weave myths about fairies and spirits around each lake and grove. Don't the trees and their shadows look strangely human in the moonlight, on a quiet evening, like a soulful congregation gazing ever upwards into the vast, mysterious Beyond? And are not the waters of the lake like quicksilver; and what better carpet than quicksilver for the feet of dancing fairies?

When they were half-way up the hill that led up to Pen y Bryn, David Hughes noticed the stars and recalled that he was profoundly interested in them, particularly when he was toiling up a steep slope, and he stopped to explain them to the Master of Pen y Bryn. He had been looking for something to take an interest in for ages; something interesting enough to compel him to stop and look at it. After all, he was out of breath. His heart leapt when he saw that it was a cloudless night.

"Are you interested in the stars, John Williams?" he asked the Master of Pen y Bryn.

"Couldn't be less interested, David Hughes," said the other, his eyes glued to the earth; "they're quite out of my world, you know."

"That's hardly surprising, since each one of them is a good deal larger than your world," said the carpenter.

"Wh-what?" exclaimed the Master of Pen y Bryn, "bigger than the world, you said? I thought they were illuminations of some kind. What do you make of the hymn, then, which goes:
'A phan y syrthio sêr y nen
Fel ffigys îr i'r llawr'.
('when the stars of heaven fall to earth like ripe figs')?"

"Well," said the carpenter, "that's what you call a metaphorical expression. The hymn-writer wasn't much of an astronomer, you see."

"You don't say," said the Master of Pen y Bryn. By this time he had started looking upwards too, and at that moment a star shot across the sky and extinguished itself on the horizon, over the farm they called Y Foty.

"What do you make of shooting stars?" he asked the carpenter; "are they bigger than this earth? They don't look much bigger than sparks from an anvil."

David Hughes could not explain shooting stars. All he knew was how to point out the North Star; so, to preserve his reputation, he hastened to perform the task at which he was expert.

"See those over there?" he said. "That's the Plough."

"The Plough?" said the Master of Pen y Bryn, livening up considerably. "Where is it?" Stars might be out of his world; a plough was not David Hughes told him all about the Plough, which was formed of stars in the sky, and how you could see the North Star if you followed the line of its blade upwards.

"Well, I never!" exclaimed the Master of Pen y Bryn, "you're absolutely right at that," and he stopped to gaze at the Plough, seeing if he could use the other stars to create something like a man's shape between its handles. If there was a man up there, did he feel he was getting old too, he wondered? Man is always ready to weave his own sorrows into the structure of the universe.

David Hughes had got his breath back by now, and was beginning to feel chilly after sweating so much, so he lost interest in the stars. But he had, without thinking, touched on a facet of the other's personality which he had not dreamed of at the time. The Master of Pen y Bryn insisted on staying a little longer to look at the Plough and the North Star, searching for a man's shape between its handles and asking himself whether he, if he existed, was perhaps getting old. And he discovered for the first time in his life, from the North Star, that Pen y Bryn faced due east. After that, he scarcely said a word all the way home; the mystery of the vast universe had begun to dawn in his soul, and he withdrew into himself to enquire whether the Ploughman was getting old; for he was absolutely certain, now, that the man was real. He thought of the days of his own youth, when even the farmyard and the little field below the house were vast territories to him. He slackened his pace, gazed around him in bewilderment, and said nothing. The carpenter had no objection to the slow pace, but he was not so keen on the silence; he was bursting with advice; and all he needed was the problem. However, the Master of Pen y Bryn was not a man you could draw out by brute force; you had to coax him to open out as the sun coaxes the daisy, and David Hughes knew that well enough. So *he* was silent, too, and he felt he was atoning a little for his snail pace.

The Master of Pen y Bryn found his mind wandering to his earliest recollections of that road. He remembered coming out of school — the school had been founded by a Congregationalist minister in the parish — and seeing, for the first time, as saplings, the tall poplars that now swayed, pale and dreamy, between him and the house. He remembered the windows of the house in the moonlight, like bright eyes alternately opening and closing according to the sway of the trees. He was overcome by his vision and he was a small child again, his years and his decrepitude forgotten. He could visualise himself dancing for joy when he saw that his father had dared to change the old plunging churn for a horse-operated churn; he marvelled at the complexity of the device, which was quite new-fangled at that time, and at his father's enterprise and wealth; for nobody else in the neighbourhood had one. He remembered how he thrilled through and through when he was allowed to mount a real live horse instead of a wooden one in the form of a broomstick; and what a marvellous thrill it was! As he approached the house and passed under the trees, the old fear returned. He had carved his name on every tree, then; during the day they were his friends, who sheltered him and played with him, but at night they were his enemies, scowling at him and thirsting for his blood. He listened to the stream flowing through the meadow, and half expected to see the paper boat he had lost many years ago caught in some hidden piece of turf; and himself gone right into the water to free it, just as he'd done many times before that, and after that too, when he fished for tadpoles. He walked past the circle which at that time, just as at this moment, he regarded as a fairy dancing ring; but it had been just a ring of toadstools for a very, very long time. When they reached the farmyard, he stopped suddenly to listen to another sound, one which used to terrify him in the old days whenever he ventured out at twilight. The countryside was absolutely silent. Nothing moved. The poplars in front of the house were still now, and the calm light of the moon smiled through their branches. There was no sound except for the cows chewing the cud and their chains grating lazily up and down the tethering posts; the rustle of hay and champing of horses as they tugged it down from the racks in the stables; an occasional hen ruffling her wings uneasily in sleep; and an owl hooting in the wood, defying herenemies to show themselves if they were in the vicinity. And in the wood, too, you could hear the occasional crackling of dry branches, as if some living creature were walking through them.

"Oh merciful heaven!" the Master of Pen y Bryn said aloud, "to think of leaving this, of all places in the world!" A sudden noise at his side brought him to his senses. David Hughes was striking a match to light his pipe; he was tired of biting his nails to kill time. When the Master of Pen y Bryn turned towards him, he saw that he, too, was thoughtful; for those last words, inspired by the magic of that evening, had given David Hughes his first inkling of the reason for his being invited home that night.

The Master of Pen y Bryn awoke from his dream, biting his tongue. "Come in, David Hughes," he said roughly, "what are you standing there for?" He did not have to address anyone else, because the third member of the company had long since vanished.

Jane Williams, the mistress of Pen y Bryn, opened the door to welcome them. Her squat, genial, hearty frame filled the doorway. Jane Williams was a round female in every sense; her face was round, her eyes were round, her mouth was round and her figure was round. When she spoke, you felt that if her voice could be transmitted to paper, just as primitive man converted the sounds he made to written symbols, it would be best represented by a perfect circle. In short, she was like a small child's picture of a human being — drawn at that stage of his development when he tries to portray everything with circles. A pair of spectacles perched on Jane Williams' round nose, and no one ever saw her look through them. She invariably looked over them, and inevitably her eyes grew round as a result, Asked why she looked over them, she would explain that they were reading glasses, which was a plausible explanation as Jane Williams was hardly an enthusiastic reader. This manner of contemplating the world made the top half of her face look like two round windows with the upper part open, like the ones you found in chapels in the old days. Jane Williams had been pretty once, and a few solitary traces of that beauty were still etched in some lines of the face, just as a few green branches are left here and there to break the monochrome of the winter landscape. Jane Williams was a genial and hospitable woman by nature, as you would expect from the look of her, and David Hughes got a warm welcome. For apart from being naturally hospitable, she shared her husband's secrets that evening, and had a high opinion of David Hughes and his advice.

The Master of Pen y Bryn and David Hughes sat on either side of the fire and looked into it, the former thinking of a way to put his story over and the latter trying to guess what it was. The only sounds that intruded on the silence were the incessant, eager plate-scraping on the part of the manservants who were finishing their supper; Annie, the daughter of the house, cutting bread and butter; and Jane's heavy breathing as she prepared the meal. And these are always pleasant, harmonious sounds.

Soon they were called to supper. David Hughes got up to make for the table somewhat hastily, and banged his head on the oak mantelpiece, so that he was again in a position to lecture on the stars — brand new ones, and all shooting stars. There was nothing static or reliable about a single one of them, like the North Star, to help him find his bearings. His tender sensibilities had to be mollified, and a bit of goose grease rubbed into the bruise, whereupon they all sat at table and began to eat. Half-way through supper, the Master of Pen y Bryn turned to David Hughes and said in a brusque, harsh tone, as if he were about to pass sentence on him: "David Hughes, I want a word of advice. I feel I'm getting too old to go on farming, and I can't decide what to do." David Hughes would have been astonished had it not been for the exclamation that the Master of Pen y Bryn had let slip in the yard, when he was lost in thought there a few minutes previously. He had given a clear indication, then, that his mind was already made up. As for Jane Williams, she had been cursed with swollen feet for years. "Yes, my dear David Hughes," she said, trying to set the ball rolling, "I keep telling him to give up farming so that we can go and live in a cottage on the little money we have. My feet get swollen something terrible, mornings especially."

David Hughes gazed, bewildered and solemn, at a damson stone on the edge of his plate, as if he were trying to solve the problem of its existence. He gazed at it for a long time, and

John and Jane Williams looked at *him*; the former chewed the end of his knife and the latter chewed the end of her apron.

"Well," said David Hughes at last, "this is rather a complex matter, John Williams; what d'you intend doing about the farm?"

"That's what I want to know," said the Master of Pen y Bryn; "what's best to do about it. I wouldn't like it to leave the family; but our Annie and our Lizzie haven't settled down yet."

David Hughes had another bout of meditation, fixing his gaze on the damson stone, and said: "I'll call again in a day or two, John Williams; I'll have had time to think it over then." They all agreed. They had a smoke and a chat and David Hughes went off home.

"It's a fine evening, John Williams," he said on his way out; "tell me, when are we going to make arrangements for the harvest thanksgiving?"

"They haven't had it at the Foty yet," said Jane Williams before her husband could reply; "they're always the last."

"Quite," said David Hughes. "There's obviously some truth in the old rhyme:

'Fe gysgodd Shôn y Foty
Ryw hanner awr ry hir.'

('Shôn Y Foty overslept by about half an hour')".

"He's a card, is David Hughes," Jane said when he had gone.

"I didn't like the way he stared at that damson stone," said her husband. "I'll go and have a chat with Mathew Thomas tomorrow night."

The Master of Pen y Bryn had been stricken in his most vulnerable spot; he could see that David Hughes was going to give him some advice which was different from his own, and he gave vent to his emotions by putting the blame on the damson stone and looking for a more naïve adviser.

On his way home that night, David Hughes heard the occasional crackle of dry branches, followed by a rustle in the hedge. He looked around him, and who should it be, sitting calmly at the roadside, but Hugh from Pant yr Afon. Hugh was a great, clumsy, harmless lout; he talked like a two-year-old and subsisted on rural charity. He could predict the future — when there was likely to be a club dinner, a new threshing machine, an auction, a wedding or a funeral, before anybody else had dreamed of it.

"Hugh," said David Hughes, "what on earth d'you think you're doing here?"

"He, he, he," said Hugh, pointing towards Pen y Bryn and winking, "a sale, a sale." He then pointed eagerly at his mouth, indicating that if *he* had said so, an auction there would be.

On the way home, David Hughes marvelled at Hugh. He took advantage of what he had said to decide, finally, what his reply to the Master of Pen y Bryn would be.

Chapter II

The following evening, Mathew Thomas was sitting calmly and quietly at home — in Y Pant, in the furthest corner of Peilliad Valley. It was half-past-eight. His main preoccupation at this moment was to admire — through rings of smoke — the chubby flesh of his youngest son Jimmy. Mathew Thomas was a gentle person; his voice was gentle, his countenance was gentle and he had a gentle manner. There are very few like him in the world; his expression radiated such a quiet gentleness that the person looking at him could not possibly object to kissing him. He was quite a short man, who stooped a little, and had one shoulder higher than the other — the result of a fall years ago from the top of a load of hay, when he was at Pen y Bryn. When he had recovered sufficiently to get around, he saw that farm labouring was too arduous for him, and he looked for a job cleaning the highway — "an end of the road job," as he put it. Be that as it may, it was enough to keep the wolf from the door and his family happy.

There was not much gossip about him. "Mathew Thomas"; no one ever said any more or any less of him. But when you had said "Mathew Thomas" you had said everything.

Mathew Thomas had an instinctive respect for farmers; he raised his cap to them every time they passed him on the road. In chapel, he was Mathew Thomas: no more, no less. In the fellowship meetings, he drew exclusively on his own experience. His constant aim, he said, was to cling to *Him*, and to dwell closer to *Him* as long as *He* saw fit to let him stay on earth. And *He* was the Almighty. Mathew Thomas never referred to the Almighty by name; he always called him *He*, just like a loving wife might talk about her dear spouse — never dreaming that anyone could possibly doubt who *He* was. Mathew Thomas was like that. It did not occur to him that anyone could suppose, when he talked about *Him*, that he meant anyone but the Almighty, and he would never have dreamed of saying *He* either if he did not know that they were pretty closely related. In Sunday school, his explanations of verses in the Bible were never very brilliant, but he could identify the *He* in the verse when *He* referred to Jesus Christ. Mathew Thomas always knew, by sheer instinct, when *He* stood for the Saviour. He could never "let rip" when he was on his knees. There were just two notes in his voice; two very pleasant notes, but still only two, and he crooned from one note to the other. He never stormed Heaven, so to speak, but he always managed to make the congregation feel that it was there. He addressed the heavenly throne as if he were having a quiet evening's chat after the day's work. There was a kind of reverence in his voice and his bearing which sprang from a deeply-ingrained habit of obedience and respect towards his masters in the flesh.

When people closed their eyes to listen to him, they visualised Mathew Thomas, cap in hand, talking to the Almighty. True, his voice and bearing betrayed respect for authority, but they also revealed that faith and confidence you notice in an old farm labourer who has stayed in one place for years, till he becomes a part of the farm, and an acknowledged member of the family. As for the two notes in his voice, they were like the bubbling waters of the brook in Peilliad Valley; and quite often, when Mathew Thomas had been "at it," whoever followed him would announce the hymn

"Ffrydiau tawel, byw, rhedegog,
O dan riniog tŷ fy Nuw,"

("quiet, living, flowing streams, beneath the threshold of the house of my God.")

Without realizing that he had chosen the hymn under Mathew Thomas' influence. The hills were not cleft asunder, and the earth did not tremble when he prayed, but he understood the secret of the dew. And you never see the dew unless the heavens are clear.

Mathew Thomas had never been a council or committee member. No one ever asked his opinion on any complicated question; and if he had been asked he would not have expressed any opinion other than that of the questioner. For this reason, he always felt awkward and uncomfortable when people had violent disagreements, and he could not feel absolutely free and easy except when he was at home amongst his own family. It was a large family.

On this particular night he sat quietly admiring, through rings of smoke, the chubby flesh of his youngest son Jimmy. Jimmy was about three and a half. He, too, was sitting in front of the fire on what was termed "the hearthrug". The hearthrug was made of sacking, and the words HENRY TATE AND SON, SUGAR REFINERS, were printed on it in big letters. Despite the material, it was clean, and that was enough for Mathew Thomas and his wife. It was warm, too, and that was enough for Jimmy; he was sitting on it stark naked, apart from a microscopic shirt that reached half way down his back. Sarah Ann Thomas, Mathew's wife, sat opposite him on the wooden settle, sewing. She was about the same age as he, but her hair had grown prematurely white, and her face was more harsh and melancholy. Jimmy was the youngest. But he had not been the youngest a year ago, which was why Sarah Ann Thomas' face was harsh and melancholy and her hair was white.

Her intellect was stronger than her husband's, so the storm had touched her more deeply. He bent down like a poplar tree, and straightened up again when the storm had passed. But she refused to bend, like an oak, and some of the branches cracked in the tempest.

Grandmother sat beside her, staring sourly into the fire, and Jimmy shot indignant glances at her from time to time. Jimmy and his grandmother were not on good terms, obviously. He seemed to be in a brown study, which in fact he was. One problem that worried him was, whether he was as much of a man as certain recent circumstances had led him to believe. He noticed that his father's shirt, which he could see through the opening in his waistcoat, buttoned up the front, and his father was definitely a man; but his own shirt buttoned up the back. The other problem was, whether his mother's present activity was an insult or a compliment as far as he was concerned. His mother was altering Peter's old suit — Peter was the next eldest brother — to fit him; the suit had been Mathew's, *his* elder brother, before that. There was about three years between each of them. Three years is an awkward interval between poor brothers; one grows out of his clothes before the other grows into them.

Jimmy sometimes felt that it was a great honour to have the suit for himself. For one thing, this was his first suit ever, and secondly, Mathew had once worn it. He hero-worshipped Mathew because he had begun to earn his own living. He got a regular twopence every Saturday for carrying water for Betsy Smith, and Betsy Smith queened it over the district. She wore a hat; everyone else of her age wore a bonnet. And she carried a parasol when it was fine, too. So Mathew Thomas' family felt that Mathew, the son, had a bright future in store, if Betsy Smith — or, rather, Mrs. Smith — took an interest in him. Jimmy was old enough to feel that he was basking in Mathew's reflected glory.

But what made him doubt whether wearing the suit was, after all, such an honour was the recollection that his full name was James Elias Thomas, or — as he recited his name to strangers when he hoped to get a penny for the performance — Dames Elaiys Thomas. The honour of being called "Elias" had not yet begun to pall. A fortnight had passed since he heard that this word was a part of his name, and he had been shown a picture of Elias near the river of Kisson, in a multicoloured garment, killing prophets for all he was worth.

This is how it was. His grandmother was an old relic of bygone days when smoking a pipe and taking a pinch of snuff were common habits among women who had not been saved. Now that she had come to spend her old age in Mathew Thomas' house, her daughter allowed her a pinch of snuff, but smoking was out. The old girl was tormented by the craving from time to time. One Sunday afternoon, a fortnight previously, she was attacked by the urge, and it was so strong that some diplomatic tactics were immediately called for. She was most genial at the tea table that afternoon, and she volunteered to look after Jimmy while everyone else went to chapel. Mr. Roberts, the minister, was officiating, and everyone was dying to hear him, but it would be difficult to keep Jimmy's mind on the afterlife and suchlike throughout the service. So it was agreed that Jimmy and his grandmother should stay at home.

When they had all gone, grannie took the great illustrated Bible from among her hidden treasures at the bottom of an old chest which was her pride and joy. Having decided that Jimmy was now old enough to keep a secret, she promised him that he could look at the pictures in the big Bible provided he didn't tell his mother or father that she had been smoking his father's tobacco while they were all in chapel. Jimmy promised eagerly, and so the dual performance began: one of them smoking and giving a running commentary on the pictures, the other overcome by the marvel of it all. He was shown the picture of Elias killing prophets, and was told that Elias was a part of his name; and he made an immediate vow that when he grew up he would not work on the road like his father, as he had once intended, but that his job would be killing prophets. She showed him a picture of the Day of Judgement, with Jesus Christ sitting on a cloud smiling at a congregation of people who looked, to him, as if they had just leapt out of bed and had not begun to get dressed. On the other side of the picture mobs of devils were tormenting great multitudes of people who were perfectly respectable as far as he could see; and his grandmother informed him that he would be among the number of the tormented if he told on her.

Jimmy swore a second time, his throat dry with fear, that he would never tell, never. Jimmy went to bed when the family came back, and shut his eyes tight so that he would not see the devils. He was asleep when his parents came into the room.

But at about three in the morning, there was an unearthly screech from Jimmy's part of the room. His mother leapt out of bed and lit a candle. He was sitting up in bed, white as a sheet, sweating profusely and screaming his head off. His mother tried to calm him. He quietened down a little and she was able to question him. She managed to make out the words "day of judgement" and "devils". His mother was frightened. She never imagined that her youngest son had ever heard that last ominous word. Grandmother's explanation was that this was an outbreak of original sin. But when Jimmy got his breath back he spilled out the whole tale, forgetting his promise, which was why, on this particular night, he was indignant with his grannie and she was looking sour. He soon forgot the Day of Judgement picture, since his mother's interpretation of it was different from his grandmother's, but he could not get Elias out of his mind. So as he sat on the hearthrug he was trying to decide whether Mathew's and Peter's old suit was worthy of him as a slayer of prophets; after all, his predecessor's suit had all the colours of the rainbow.

To repeat: Jimmy was not Mathew Thomas' only child. He had five, and each of them was busy with some task or other as their father sat admiring Jimmy's chubby flesh and their mother sat making his first suit. Next to Jimmy sat Peter, his brother, and it was obvious that Peter was learning to read at school, since he was amusing himself by trying to read the hearthrug. First he would quietly spell out a word, and when he was sure of it he would shout it out with all his might, like H-E-N-R-Y, Hendry, and so on; just like a child who steps gingerly on the ice to begin with and, seeing that it is going to hold, rushes ahead with all the force he can muster. Having succeeded in spelling the name, he racked his brain as to why people spelt Hendry without a "d", since the word had always been Hendry as far as he was concerned.

Mathew was standing on a chair gazing into a scrap of looking glass trying to work out the number of ways a human being can arrange his features and still manage to recognise himself. Lewis sat at the corner of a table, trying out a mouth-organ he'd got that day at school in exchange for a ninety-cuckoo conker. Conkers came into their own at this time of year. Perhaps I should explain to the unititiated what a ninety-cuckoo conker is. You make a hole in the shell of a chestnut, and draw a string through it, and there's your conker. This is how you play conkers. You put your cap on the ground, and one boy puts his chestnut on it, and his opponent tries to break it with *his* conker, and so on in turns until one nut is broken. The winner is a cuckoo-one conker. If the broken one was a cuckoo something, say cuckoo five, then the winner would be cuckoo six because, having vanquished the other nut, it would take over its spoils. It will be realised that a ninety-cuckoo conker is pretty valuable; and if you find one of these you usually find something stronger than air — pitch, usually — inside it. So Lewis' conker was worth a mouth organ at least.

There was another brother present, but he was invisible for the time being. This was Moses, who was fourteen. Moses felt that he was fast becoming a man. The Sunday evening previously he had decided not to go forward and recite a verse in chapel. His mother ordered him to go, and he refused. His mother could not force him in front of everyone, so she compromised by giving him a hefty pinch in the arm. Moses found this very painful, and he was currently sitting behind the wooden settle, his coat discarded and his sleeves rolled up, seeing whether the wound was likely to prove fatal. Their sister, Sarah Jane, was there too. She was standing on a chair studying the picture of a handsome lad on the wall, all ringlets and curls. He was a distant relation; the children had seen him once or twice and they called him Charlie North of England. This was their mother's name for him. No one ever called him anything else and no one knew where the North of England was.

The other objects on the wall were "The Cloud of Witnesses", the picture of the local squire, the battle of Waterloo, an almanac bearing the picture of a small child of about a year old playing with a cat (the family were very interested in any small child of a year old), a birch rod and a bunch of sage. These will provide a fair image of Mathew Thomas and his family at this time. Obviously, none of them was dreaming of a visitor that night, and a visitor up in Peilliad Valley after nightfall was a rare occurrence indeed. There was yet another indication that they expected to spend the rest of the evening on their own. Four red herrings were frying gaily in front of the fire, and spitting mockingly into it. I can say with the Psalmist: "I have been young and now am old,' but I have never yet met anyone who didn't like red herrings, nor have I ever met anyone who was willing to admit it. For this reason, the ceremony of eating them is deferred to some evening when no one outside the family is expected. The secret — that everyone likes them — is shared across the table, and this engenders a certain peace and mutual understanding which reigns supreme, and which the world knows nothing of.

So the family were enjoying their evening together, and Mathew Thomas was enjoying a quiet smoke in his chair, smiling benevolently at each one in turn. There was a knock at the door. It was John Williams, the Master of Pen y Bryn, who entered, without waiting for anyone to open. "Hello," he said, "you haven't got company then?" And indeed Mathew Thomas and his wife, and his wife's mother, had no company when the Master of Pen y Bryn opened the door. Mathew Thomas leapt to his feet and gave him a kind of half bow; Sarah Ann Thomas, too, jumped up and curtsied.

"Where are the children," asked the Master of Pen y Bryn, "in bed, I suppose?"

No one answered him, since Sarah Ann Thomas was flustered and trying to gather up her sewing, and Mathew was trying to find him a place to sit, and the old woman was trying to hide the herrings. In a moment, the Master of Pen y Bryn could see that the children were quite near, for he noticed the tip of a nose and a crown of hair emerging over the top of the settle, and an eye peeping-out from under a chair, and the sound of a suppressed sigh. The sigh came from Jimmy; he was too young to be diplomatic. Eventually, the Master of Pen y Bryn asked Mathew Thomas to come back with him a little way, and when he got him outside he told him what he had to say. He did not have to tell him to keep the secret, for Mathew Thomas was dependable as a rock; he knew that. He appealed to him as an old workman of his who knew Pen y Bryn well.

"I'm getting old, Mathew," said the Master of Pen y Bryn.

"Very good, sir," said Mathew, touching his cap.

"And decrepit," said the Master of Pen y Bryn.

"Very good, sir," said Mathew innocently. He preferred to agree with his old master that he looked old and decrepit, however much pain that might give his master, to crossing him in any way. And Mathew Thomas chose to agree with his old master even when he was shamming, rather than venture to cross him. There was so much of the servitor in him that he saw nothing strange in this.

"I'm thinking of giving up farming," said the Master of Pen y Bryn.

"Very good, sir," said Mathew.

"And going to live on the little that I have," said the other.

"Very good, sir," said Mathew again, without removing his finger from his cap. The Master of Pen y Bryn knew him too well to expect anything else.

He said good night to him and went off home, more determined than ever to give up the farm. He felt grateful that there was one wise man in the neighbourhood apart from himself — and that wise man was Mathew Thomas.

Just as the Master of Pen y Bryn was knocking at Mathew Thomas' door, David Hughes, the carpenter, was knocking at the door of Y Ddôl, where Robin's father lived. When he had got his breath he said, *sotto voce* — though that was hardly necessary since Richard Hughes, his brother, was alone in the house — "Do you want a bigger farm, Dick?"

"Is there one going?" asked Richard Hughes.

"No," said David, "but there will be, if you want a farm."

"Whose land," asked Richard; "Sir John's or the bishop's?"

"The bishop's," said David Hughes.

Chapter III

The Master of Pen y Bryn was neither old nor decrepit. It was a matter of feeling, and the feeling was engendered by a number of circumstances, all significant to someone as touchy as he. He felt that nature had never intended him to be a farmer. The craft most likely to suit him was that of a gentleman, and no one was more convinced of this than himself. When he was young, no handsomer lad ever stood on Llangeunant bridge on a Sunday morning. All the local youths used to congregate there, summer and winter, to put the world to rights. He was a tall lad, straight as a shaft of light, his luxuriant auburn hair parted meticulously on the right and brushed back. For some reason he was obsessed with the idea that people who parted their hair on the right were cleverer than those who parted it on the left.

At that period, he might have been mistaken for a budding musician, a doctor or an aspirant to the ministry. The only objection to the latter supposition was that his walk was too sprightly and his expression too serene; he did not look as if he carried all the sins of the world on his shoulders. When he was a child his parents thought of making a musician of him, and they took him to the conductor of Bethania choir to test his voice and his talent. The conductor took him alone into a room and asked him which song he knew best, and he said The Men of Harlech. At that time the village band was learning "The Men of Harlech" and everybody you passed in the street was humming it. There was not a soul, young or old, who did not hum "The Men of Harlech" as he ploughed the land, or milked the cows, or walked, or rode a horse. The whole of life, in those days, was tuned in to "The Men of Harlech". It was to the beat of this song that every domestic animal worked, ran or walked, and it was rare to find a rabbit crossing the road to any other.

So no wonder John Williams, the Pen y Bryn lad, said that he knew "The Men of Harlech" better than any other song and let his fate as a musician hang on it.

The Bethania choirmaster sat himself comfortably in an armchair and ordered him to start. When he was half-way through the first line, he stopped him for being off key. He started again and was stopped again — in the middle of the first line. He started a third time — this time the conductor had pitched the right note for him — but he was in dire trouble before the end of the first line. The fourth time, he started with the other conducting him, and he got through the first line without a hitch, and when he realised that he had started on the second without disaster he lifted up both heart and voice. But he had barely placed a foot on the threshold, as it were, than he stumbled again, and since he had no other tune in mind he had to start "The Men of Harlech" all over again. He was wishing by now that the Men of Harlech had never existed, never gone to war and never won a battle.

He went back to the beginning, and to his surprise he was allowed to get through the third line without being stopped, and the fourth, and the fifth, and the sixth. He was in full swing by now and ended on a note of triumph, full of admiration for the Men of Harlech and their heroism. He turned to the choirmaster for the praise he deserved. The other was just beginning to get his breath back, after laughing till he was black in the face. He was half lying in his chair, his hands on his sides, shaking from head to foot. That was John Williams' first impression of him when he had finished singing. He thought he had fainted at first, but he heard him draw powerful, rapid breaths, like a cart running downhill with a brake on its wheel. The conductor laughed, a long, hearty, expansive laugh, with all the force of his lungs. When he came to he informed John Williams that whatever talent he had been blessed with, it was not musical.

After that John Williams was apprenticed to a shopkeeper, but in three months he brought a note home from his boss saying that he was a quiet, obedient boy, but that he would never make a shopkeeper. His mother, so she said later, had heard during those three months that his master was rather a feckless fellow, and when young John brought the note home she naturally maintained that the boss did not know what the qualities necessary for a good shopkeeper were. He got a place with another shopkeeper, the best shop in Coeadarglodd town, on the strength of his father's status as a farmer. But in about three months John came home again with a note saying he was a pleasant, polite lad, but that he would never make a shopkeeper.

His parents were pretty depressed by now, but John had a ray of comfort to give them. During his three months in Coedarglodd he developed a pimple on the side of his nose, and this caused him a lot of mental torment. He was as fussy about his skin as he was about his hair, and he was very fussy about both. He thought everybody was looking at his nose as he walked along the street. Whenever he saw a young girl coming along, who was likely to pass on the side of the pimple, he would cross the street so that she would only see him from the good side of his nose, and find him attractive. He was searching around in a corner one evening, after sweeping out the shop at the end of the day, and he came across a panphlet about some infallible remedy for just about everything. Amongst the illustrations was one of a lad with two or three pimples on his nose and three or four dozen on the rest of his face. Under the picture was the lad's own testimony, signed by himself, that the remedy advertised had cured him, so that his skin was smooth as a babe's in less than a week. The pamphlet gave all sorts of weird information about the composition of the human body, its functions, and the ills it was heir to, and there was a detailed explanation of the growth of pimples. You were urged to see whether you had anything like black thorns in the skin of your face, and if you had, your blood was unhealthy, and the ground was fertile for pimples.

Before going to bed that night John looked for the black thorns for quite a while in the glass, and he came across quite a few — particularly at the base of his nose. He had a bright idea. He thought it would be a good thing to squeeze them out before they developed, and he spent quite a long time on the task. Some time during the night he woke to find his nose smarting terribly, and he discovered that it was much thicker than usual. When he got up in the morning his nose was huge and inflamed, and John, behind it, felt ashamed to show himself. That day at the shop was a failure, one of the days that contributed generously to the despatch of the letter describing John's general uselessness as a shopkeeper. In the days that followed he thought a great deal about the causes of spots and blackheads. He read copiously about them in every pamphlet he came across. All these snippets of knowledge were absolutely fascinating. Among other things, he became an authority on hair growth and the causes of its degeneration, and the causes of blackheads and spots, and that was quite a lot of knowledge for a lad of fifteen.

He gave much more time to these studies than to his work at the shop, and he wondered how he could find more time to study them. Suddenly, it dawned on him that it would be an excellent idea to become a doctor. The ray of comfort he shed on his parents, then, was the mention of this possibility, when he brought them back that last note saying he would never succeed in business.

A week after he arrived home in disgrace from Coedarglodd, he was engaged, as a kind of servant, by Dr. Griffiths, Llan Gain. This was a small town some six miles away, with only a row of hills stretching between it and Llangeunant. It was to Llan Gain that the farmers took their produce every week, so John could see his parents there often. He loved it there. He no longer read pamphlets on pimples and hair roots, but long articles supported by scientific illustrations. In due course he learned all there was to know about them — and enough to know that there was no cure for baldness. There were other subjects a doctor had to master which he had not bargained for, and as he tried to master them each new piece of information had a strange effect on him. He imagined himself prey to every illness he studied. If the liver was under discussion, he would spend half his time in front of the glass scrutinising his tongue and the whites of his eyes; if he were studying tuberculosis, he would stay awake for a long time after going to bed to see if he suffered from night sweating. In the end he actually began to look ill, and the doctor sent him home for some fresh air, with a note to say that although he took a great interest in his work, being a doctor did not agree with him. John stayed at home for a very long time, helping on the farm, escorting nervous young ladies after nightfall, and generally mooching around. There was only one honourable profession left which he and his parents could think of now — and something had to be found for him, because he was now about twenty — and that was the profession of preacher.

The decision was made. All the theological books in the house were rooted out, which did not take long, and he began studying them. His father brushed up his own meagre bit of theology to help his son, and they studied hard for ages, till John felt himself able to detect theological errors in the sermons of the ministers and lay preachers who came, from Sunday to Sunday, to preach in Llangeunant. There was nothing ominous about this; it is a disease which attacks most lads of eighteen or twenty in their turn. He now had three major activities. He would spend the day in the fields trying to get his colour back, and every other night at home studying theology or preaching to the rats and mice in the hayloft, trying to convince them that they were sinful and beyond redemption. That is, whenever the labourers happened to go down to the village for a walk. He wrote a sermon. He knew that he would probably have to preach his first sermon in the presence of some preacher or other, and he was determined to make the occasion as much like a big meeting as possible, so he began his first written sermon formally, like this: "A few more minutes only before we hear our beloved brother." The ending was every bit as orthodox: "May the Lord be with His beloved servant in his message, for His Name's sake, Amen." He practised the pitch and tone of this last sentence, and so he was finally ready for the pulpit.

The time came to have a chat with the minister; it was decided that his father should be the one to go and proclaim the worthy intentions of his son John. But on the evening John asked his father to put the visit off for a while. The father agreed; after all, his son knew his own business best. In the meantime John himself went and told the minister, not that he wanted to start preaching but that he was going to marry Jane, the daughter of William and Mary Roberts of Pant y Gwair. She was a charming young girl with more than average good looks. He told his parents the same story when he got home. In the circumstances, he could not get married *and* start preaching, so there was nothing for it but to make the most of a bad job.

His father rented another little farm apart from Pen y Bryn — Y Ddôl, and since John knew more about farming than anything else he and his wife Jane were ensconced there. The story was the talk of the neighbourhood for a while, but there was no particular alarm or despondency. John and Jane kept away from fellowship meetings of their own accord, and they were received back without trouble as full members within three months — soon after they got married.

Before long there was another similar occurrence in the neighbourhood; the thing was forgotten and John and Jane Williams were able to cast off their shame. They took a prominent part in religious services, and were proudly conscious of being the handsomest pair worshipping at Bethania. John Williams' hair shone as brightly as ever, and his skin was as smooth as ever, and Jane Williams was wholesome and attractive to look at. Annie, their little girl, had inherited the combined good looks of both. John Williams revelled in his youth and good fortune for some years; but one morning he fancied

— surely it was nothing but fancy? that his hair was getting thinner on top. He grew pale, and kept the secret to himself. He examined his head meticulously, and found reason to believe that the baldness was spreading pretty drastically. After that, he made a point of staying in bed later than his wife, so that every day he could find a surreptitious opportunity to probe the consequences of the catastrophe. Old age shuddered icily through him and he lost his genial manner. Gradually, his voice acquired an unprecedented squeak, the wrinkles multiplied on his face, and life lost its glory and its romance for him.

As he grew thinner his wife got fatter; they found they were a middle-aged couple, and still living in Y Ddôl. Y Ddôl was a fine farm for a young couple starting life together, but for a middle-aged, well-off couple it was no great shakes. John Williams' youth had faded early, and he could not revive it; so he began to cast an eye on his father's home, Pen y Bryn. At long last, the old couple retired from Pen y Bryn and went to live in Glan yr Afon, a house built by John Williams' father to provide for his old age; and John Williams Y Ddôl and his wife became the master and mistress of Pen y Bryn — a farm worthy of their pretentions though too good for their farming abilities. John Williams Y Ddôl became Mr. Williams, Pen y Bryn, an official of Bethania chapel, a member of the local committees and, eventually, justice of the peace. The hedges of Pen y Bryn grew progressively more untidy, and you can judge a farmer's character by the state of his hedges. It was enough for Mr. Williams — so he said — to be in charge of Pen y Bryn, and he gave Y Ddôl over completely to someone else's charge.

Pen y Bryn was still a good farm, albeit a farm that had lost its glory. The son found it a far tougher business to keep Pen y Bryn in order than Y Ddôl. His heart was not in his work; so there were many occasions when he felt that life was a burden. He longed for the time when he could attain the state he thought nature intended for him — that of a gentleman. He indulged in dreams and fantasies about it; and his visions were such as could not be incorporated into meadows and animals. The visions were — the different varieties of gentlemen.

Chapter IV

It was seven o'clock on a fine morning towards the end of September. However, there was already a row of carriages and carts on Llangeunant Bridge, and the sound of children yelling and pigs screeching and hens and ducks clucking and quacking till the countryside resounded. Some of the children were standing quietly on the bridge, in their Sunday best, leaning on the handrail like a row of statues. Others, in their everyday clothes, were running between the carriages and the carts, pulling the pigs' tails and the feathers of the poultry, and screaming their heads off to make themselves heard. Every now and then they would troop back in a procession to the bridge, to make fun of the children of privilege — verbally, that is: at heart they admired them. These were the underprivileged. After each excursion to the bridge, someone from the silent row of children would inevitably break down. His collar or clothes would be pelted with dirt; his handkerchief would get stolen; a nice, clean cap would be hurled into the ditch — or his family nickname would be thrown in his face, and he in his best clothes too. It is much easier to bear the brunt of the family nicknames in your everyday clothes than in your Sunday best. What with the mockery of the underprivileged, the mud-slinging, and everything else, the congregation of the blessed would look pretty sorry for themselves by starting time.

It was the day of Llan Gain fair, and the silent crowd on the bridge were the chosen ones who were going; the unruly mob consisted of the rejected.

Llan Gain fair was a big one. This was the one day of the year when everybody who had not sunk into irredeemable poverty tried to scrape enough together to go there. This particular morning, twenty minutes before the carriages were due to set out, you could see a kind of statue with a crooked shoulder on the peak of one of Llangeunant's hills, between you and the sun; and since the sun was directly behind the statue you could only see its bare outline. Three or four children danced round it like a lot of puppies let loose. One tugged at the statue's hand and another at its legs, but it was immovable. Then the children ran forward a little, then back, then forward again, waving handkerchiefs at the children on the bridge; then they folded the handkerchiefs carefully, maintaining the original fold, and put them in their pockets. Then they ran back again and tugged at the statue and danced round it. Eventually a woman appeared over the horizon, panting like a great pair of bellows. She puffed so violently that her whole body seemed to be puffing and blowing. She got to the crest of the hill and put down the infant she was carrying. The infant ran to the statue and tugged at it, and the statue moved.

Mathew Thomas, Cwm Peilliad, was the statue; the woman was Sarah Ann Thomas and she was carrying Jimmy. Mathew Thomas had been terribly preoccupied for weeks, ever since he had promised to take the family to Llan Gain fair. He was afraid of being late and missing the carriages. He had started off in front of his spouse that morning, as a gentle hint to hurry her up. He was so frightened of being left behind that when he looked over his shoulder and realised that his wife and Jimmy were not yet in sight, he became absolutely petrified on top of the hill above the village.

They got to the village, sought out the right carriage (they had reserved a place with the driver weeks before), and deposited Peter, Mathew, Moses and Sarah Jane on the bridge to swell the ranks of the blessed. They had been adjured not to chew their handkerchiefs or lose their money. It was starting time. Which was fortunate; otherwise there would have been a riot on the bridge. One of the legion of the wretched had hit

Peter with a clod of earth, and Mathew had left the ranks to settle accounts with him. The row of children got so interested in the proceedings that they forgot they were standing in a row, and formed a circle round Moses and Peter's opponent, cheering Moses on to deeds of bravery for all they were worth. Whereupon Mathew Thomas and his wife and Jimmy came to drag the rest of the family to the carriage. The congregation on the bridge jumped into their various carriages; the carriages set off; the other mob rushed off after them as fast as they could go, to spoil their prospects of a good time as much as possible. But the mob got short of breath as it ran, and consequently less articulate. After the carriages had gone the village calmed down again, and the legion of the lost disappeared as if the earth had swallowed them.

They left the village and the hills of Llan Gain began to come into view. The faces of the children in the carriages all lit up like sun after rain. They expressed an opinion on everyone and everything they passed, and everyone, old and young, tried to tell a funny story of some kind, or to display his potential wit in some other way; and everyone laughed heartily, no matter how feeble the wit. This capacity for laughing at every weak joke always manifests itself during fair time, or a Sunday school trip, or a wedding in particular. This may be because the general merriment creates a kind of generosity towards the raconteur, and a desire not to let him down. Many a man revises his own opinion of himself, even if he has never regarded himself as a wit, if he manages to send a company into convulsions of laughter on such an occasion — by means of some tame, innocent little remark laced with a tentative humour.

Gradually, the initial tumult in the carriages died down, and the older ones started chatting, *sotto voce*, about the prospects of the fair. The children were telling each other all about the things they intended to buy; a penny had tremendous possibilities. Everyone said what he would like and then Peter said he wanted to buy a "spineglass' (spying glass). All the children marvelled at Peter's enterprise. The sum he intended to pay for the telescope was one penny. The conversation was occasionally interrupted by greetings yelled by the company to everyone who passed — carts, carriages, sheep drovers and cattle drovers in abundance.

The two carts that attracted most attention were Samuel Jones Ty Glas' pig cart and the master of Pen y Bryn's pig cart. They discussed Samuel Jones and his cargo rather flippantly, and the Master of Pen y Bryn and his cart somewhat more respectfully, since Jane Williams, his wife, was in one of the carriages. As they passed Samuel Jones and his pig cart they reminisced, for the thousandth time, about something he once said at Sunday school. Samuel Jones was a good, strong man, with a deep voice like the roar of thunder in the distant hills. He interspersed every word he spoke with a sound something in between *ugh* and *er* — but rather more like the former than the latter. He was feared by children and young preachers, and loved by old people and all his friends and neighbours. This was the story everyone told when they were hard up for anything else to say about Samuel Jones.

They were discussing in Sunday school the miracle of driving the demons into the swine and curing the man who was possessed by them. Everyone pronounced his opinion; and then Samuel Jones was asked for his interpretation of the story. "Ugh, my interpretation, ugh er," said Samuel Jones in full roar, "is that the two most frightful creatures that the Almighty ever created met up — a pig and a devil, ugh er." Someone in every carriage told the story as they passed Samuel Jones that morning; everyone had heard it dozens of times but they reacted as if it were new, and they laughed at it till the countryside rang, and Mathew Thomas, too, shook with laughter under the influence of the old tale, feeling surprised at his own potential for happiness.

It may be that an old story, like old clichés from a pulpit, appeals more strongly to a rural populace than new stories and new observations, just as a man in a strange crowd is glad to see the face of an old friend. This joy at seeing the face of an old friend in a crowd of strangers is a great one, particularly for the man who does not go away from home very often. It is not often that country folk leave their own environment, either physically or spiritually, and when they do they feel uncomfortable.

"Well, well," said John Owen the cobbler by and by, "here's the Master of Pen y Bryn and his new horse," and Hugh, Pant yr Afon, doubled up with merriment at the remark. There was nothing to laugh at in this remark, true, but Hugh, who had entered into the spirit — though not the level of understanding — of the company, thought you had to laugh at everything that was said that morning. "Hush!" everyone immediately hissed at Hugh, "Mrs. Williams is in the next carriage," and Hugh crept into his shell, feeling in some obscure way that he had put his foot in it; as far as he was concerned he was just as entitled to laugh at the cobbler's remark as at any other remark that morning. This laugh of his was simply a continuation of the way he had been laughing since his christening; his face, which kept smiling even when his spirit had plumbed the dark depths, made this clear. The two were not on the same wavelength. Yes, Hugh was one of the crowd, and it would not have been complete without him. He was free to go wherever he liked, and to choose his transport. Hardly anyone understood what Hugh said, except the children. He was nearly always with the children on the local bridge, holding forth, and they understood. This particular morning, before starting, he had a great effect on them. They gazed at him, pale and solemn, as he delivered his oration, waving his arms frantically like a windmill. The gist of his *spiel* was that they should make sure to be in bed before nine o'clock that night, because he would be on the bridge then, back from Llan Gain fair, dead drunk.

The Master of Pen y Bryn's new horse was adjudicated, and the judgement was a very favourable one. Jane Williams sat there blushing, pretending not to listen, peering over her glasses more eagerly than ever. The carriage passed Pen y Bryn's cart; the men all said good morning, fingering their caps, and the girls half got up from their seats so that it would look vaguely like a curtsey when they sat down again. The children looked blank, as if they were in the presence of something quite inexplicable. It is probably as difficult to estimate exactly how much property a man should have to merit cap-touching, and curtseys, and how much to merit no more than a nod, as to divine how children know what time of year to bring out their marbles or their peg tops. But the Master of Y Ddôl "arrived" when he became the Master of Pen y Bryn and inherited his father's status.

The Master's new horse was a good one. This is why he, and not a servant, took the pigs to market. The new horse was the talk of the neighbourhood, and it was such a fine one that its owner felt he could put up with farming well enough; and he felt youth and enthusiasm coursing through his veins as he heard the comments from the carriages.

At last, they got to Llan Gain.

There, the scene was indescribable, and the sound even more so, with the cattle rushing around and lowing, the sheep slithering between the legs of the crowd and bleating, and the dogs chasing them; the drovers yelling and thumping, and a torrent of loquacity everywhere. An occasional drover whose beasts had run amuck would get so furious that he would stand in the middle of the road, his mouth open to pour out a stream of automatic and uncontrollable abuse. You could hear the music of the fair, and the noise of the 'roundabout', the pedlars of all manner of wares trying to shout each other down; the one who made the most noise got the most business. In the middle of all this you could hear farmers arguing, getting mad, pleading and nudging each other, as if they were the only ones in the whole fair. The Llangeunant coaches went to their separate tavern yards for the day, and everyone got out and went his own way.

Mathew Thomas and his wife wandered aimlessly here and there, he leading the procession, his wife and Jimmy following, Peter and Mathew next and Lewis and Moses and Sarah Jane trailing along behind *them*. Everyone livened up when they saw the Master of Pen y Bryn passing through with his pig cart and his new horse; and they greatly admired a man who regarded the crowd and the hullabaloo with such indifference. They tried to attract his attention in various ways which would not seem too bold, but all in vain, and they dragged themselves on, munching apples and cracking nuts and gazing into shop windows.

They wandered around for a bit and came to a fruit stall, and — surprise! — Jane Williams, Pen y Bryn, was standing there. They went and tried to draw her attention, to convince her that so far they had managed not to get lost or get trampled on. She approached them very kindly, gave a penny to each child, and laid a hand on Jimmy's head. Their parents ordered each one of the children to say: "Thank you, ma'am," with a stress on the "ma'am," and bow or curtsey according to their sex. Jane Williams smiled on them all and went her way. They stopped for a little while near the fruit stall to admire the endless variety of goods displayed there, but they wentoff without plucking up enough courage to buy anything.

The Master of Pen y Bryn saw the camp moving on, and he felt grateful that he was not as other men. To convince himself of this, he went into the Crown stables again to admire his new horse. He had sold his pigs at a good price, and he wanted a drink or two before starting off from the station with a load of coal. The Master of Pen y Bryn was a prominent chapelgoer, but very few people would blame him for having a glass or two in Llan Gain fair. If he drank at Llangeunant fair, that would be something quite different. The prominent chapelgoers of Llangeunant would not dream of going on the booze at the local fair, but they saw nothing wrong with doing the same at Llan Gain. And the prominent chapelgoers of Llan Gain felt just the same. They would not hesitate to strike a bargain over a glass in Llangeunant, but they would not dream of doing this at their own local fair. Did they feel there was a moral distinction between the two kinds of drinking? Yes, and an important one. The same difference that makes a man who is very fond of smoking at home, or at a neighbour's home, tremble with the fear of God if it be suggested to him that he should smoke in the street. Moral distinctions are great, clear-cut and vital in the lives of upright men.

After midday the animals and their noise receded, and the number of amusements and auctioneers increased. There was one very philanthropic auctioneer at a street corner. His job was to sell watches and the like; or rather, he was willing to pay anyone in cash who would take them off his hands, even though they were good watches. He had a paper bag, and he threw in a watch plus five shillings, and asked tenshillings for the lot. No one would buy, so he added another five shillings, and yet another, in his desire to get the reluctant audience to think of its own good. John Owen the cobbler was there, and Joe from Gwernant, and his brother Will; and the prospects of the bargain made each of them tremble — if only they could find the strength to shout! It was to this stall that Mathew Thomas and his little band came eventually; after having quite a good time, all things considered. Mathew Thomas could not understand at first what was going on, but he got a full explanation from Joe Gwernant and Will his brother. He gazed anxiously about him, but then he saw that Jane Williams, Pen y Bryn, was there, and his doubts vanished. There she was, enjoying herself hugely, her dress rucked up a bit above her waist to reveal a multicoloured garment — or perhaps a garment without any colour at all. She stood with folded arms, her spectacles on her nose, and gazed over them at the auctioneer, with a round, wide smile. Her hat was tilted towards the salesman as if her smile had pushed it to one side — she was smiling more broadly on the side furthest from the man. Her shoes were covered in mud from the streets, but she did not mind; they were good strong shoes, not "frippery little bits of nonsense".

Mathew Thomas wanted a watch to give to Moses, because Moses was beginning to come of age, and would have to leave home soon. Mathew Thomas was poor; a pound was a great deal to him. But he had ten shillings in his pocket which he had kept for the fair. He did not think that Jane Williams would be there — and surely she would not smile like that — unless the auctioneer was really a great philanthropist. Dependence on the philanthropy of others was nothing new to him. Having convinced himself that he was not giving up his money to usury — whatever that might mean — he mustered enough energy to tell the auctioneer that he wished to take advantage of his philanthropy. The auctioneer got his ten shillings, the contents of Mathew's pocket and his heart's blood, and Mathew got the paper bag and its treasure. Oddly enough, this was the last watch in stock; so there was disappointment for quite a number who, by now, had got a little bolder. Having sold this watch, there was nothing the salesman could do but pack his bags and catch the next train to get additional stock, so that he could go somewhere else and announce to some other fellow-human-beings how concerned he was about their welfare.

Mathew Thomas retreated as soon as he could to a quiet spot to investigate the paper bag; his family, John Owen the cobbler, Joe Gwernant and his brother Will followed him. He was leaping forwards at such a rate that they could only follow from a distance. When they caught him up he was standing frozen in a corner, pale as a ghost, lips trembling; he was gazing into space with the paper bag in his hand. His wife tried to get him to talk, but Mathew Thomas did not move; the only movement in his whole body was the trembling at the corners of his lips. Joe Gwernant ran to look for the salesman, and so did brother Will and John Owen the cobbler, but the train had gone. When they got back Mathew Thomas' whole family were crying round him, though he himself was not moving a finger or turning his eyes from that spot in space he was gazing at. Joe got the paper bag away from him; inside were a cheap watch and four pennies, and the fruits of Mathew's long labours, which should have gone to his children, had vanished.

He lived in Peilliad Valley, and was brought up there, secluded from the world. The world's hubbub was no more to him than a far distant, indefinable murmur, audible now and then like the murmur of the sea in a mountainous region; and it was a sweet murmur heard from a distance. This was the first time he had made contact with the world; which was why he was gazing so long into space. The world's icy finger had touched his soul. He did not know the meaning of the chill that penetrated his bones; he was psychologically incapable of grasping what had happened. He was too innocent to understand. Mathew Thomas went home stunned. He was afraid of hearing that distant murmur for a long time, lest the strange chill should penetrate his being again. And whenever that murmur happened to come up the valley now and then, on the breeze, and that indefinable chill crept over him, Mathew Thomas would go to his chair by the fireside to sit still and bewildered, staring into space.

The homeward experiences of the various travellers were pretty mixed. Some had got bargains, others losses. Some were gay, some were sad, and others moody. Of them all Mathew Thomas was the only one that seemed completely bewildered. Margaret Jones, from Rhyd Lydan, had managed to get a one-and-sixpenny cap for her husband for a shilling, she said; and she congratulated herself raucously in the carriage on the way home. Poor thing, it did not occur to her that every shopkeeper raises his price for the benefit of farmers, so that he can lower them again when they come to his shop and give them a bargain. He knows that a bargain means the world to them.

Of all the happy ones that afternoon the Master of Pen y Bryn was the happiest. He had got a good price for his pigs, everyone had congratulated him on his horse, and he had drunk enough to feel romantic. The carriages passed him; he was bringing his load of coal and singing softly to himself, and that was a good sign. But the inmates of the carriages knew nothing of the tragedy that overtook him before the end of that day, and cast a shadow on his life. That afternoon, he felt better adjusted to his work than he had ever done before, and he little imagined that in a couple of days he would be inviting David Hughes the carpenter to his home for advice about giving up farming — because of his old age and decrepitude.

This is how it happened. He was coming down the hill with his horse and his load of coal, when there was a sudden sound behind him. A cart with a load of earthenware pots, drawn by a mule, passed him like a lightning flash, the driver singing his head off in his own special fashion. The horse leapt to one side and reared, and the first thing that the Master of Pen y Bryn saw was the load of coal disappearing into the field, followed by the horse, and the slope at that side of the road was pretty steep. He stood there bewildered for a second, looking at the gap in the hedge, then he turned suddenly on his heel and walked on. Rhyd Lydan's labourer, who was busy ploughing ready for sowing wheat, saw that there was something amiss up the road, and raced towards the spot. When he got there all he could see was the Master of Pen y Bryn walking calmly towards Llangeunant, twiddling his walking stick between his fingers. He went after him, and just before he caught him up he saw him pulling a fern from the hedge. Then he sat by the roadside whistling softly, staring at the fern leaf as if he had never seen anything like it before.

"Mr. Williams," asked the Rhyd Lydan farm servant sharply, "where's the cart?"

"What did you say, my boy?" asked the Master of Pen y Bryn, slowly and feebly.

"Where's the cart?" asked the servant as if he were talking to the deaf.

"Oh," said the Master of Pen y Bryn in the same tone, "the cart is with the new horse, my lad."

"But where's the horse?"

"The new horse has gone, lad, yes the new horse has gone," he said, still in the same low key.

"Where, man?"

"Gone to the multitude," the other replied.

"What multitude?" asked the servant impatiently.

"He has passed away to the multitude on the other side," said the Master of Pen y Bryn in the same tone.

He did not raise his head as he spoke, but calmly tore off a bit of the fern leaf as he uttered each sentence, and gently kicked a stone, and he spoke in an undertone as if he were in the presence of the dead. The Rhyd Lydan lad rushed past him towards the gap he could see in the hedge, and he saw the load of coal scattered all over the field, and the cart on its side, and the horse lying there quietly, blinking up at the sky. He whistled to a fellow in the distance and between them they managed to right the cart and the horse, and put the coal back in the cart, and take them through a gate into the road. They brought them to the Master of Pen y Bryn. They shook him and showed them to him. He leapt up wildly, and looked at the horse in consternation as if it were a creature that had risen from the ashes, and he went home rejoicing. He gave each of the men half-a-crown to keep the matter quiet, but their promise could not erase the traces of coal in the field or the gap in the hedge where it had fallen. In the days that followed he encountered knowing grins from everyone he met, which made him hate farming more than ever, so much so that at the first opportunity he invited David Hughes the carpenter to Pen y Bryn to advise him, pleading old age and decrepitude. In the kind of world the Master of Pen y Bryn lived in, these petty things were great trials and tragedies.

Chapter V

It was a quiet, pleasant evening towards the end of February or the beginning of March, just before sunset. You could see the craggy range of Rhewyn between the sun and the earth — blue under the snow and the light mist that shrouded it, mist which cast a blue shadow on the snow, and yet was not thick enough to conceal it. As the sun sank and it grew dark, the fog rose on the meadows; the sheep and lambs wandered to and fro like phantoms. The countryside was intensely silent. The only movement was the strange movement of sheep in the fog, and the water under the footbridge by the Cae Mawr gate. And the only sound was the tumult of the water, and the rustling of a rabbit or two, and the twittering of an occasional bird. But as the sun was setting a blackbird began to sing, and a thrush on another branch answered, and a number of birds from the depths of the forest answered its call in their turn. The woodland chorus sang one of the first songs of this spring; it was a very shy song to begin with, as if they were not used to their audience. The song grew louder with practice, and soon promised to become deafening, but when it was on the verge of crescendo the clear, precise to-who of an owl re-echoed over the landscape, and the choir fell silent in the twinkling of an eye — so suddenly that you could hear the echo of the owl's cry from a neighbouring rock.

In a while, a feeble cry broke the silence. It was the cry of a sickly lamb in Cae Mawr nearby; he had just experienced the cold world for the first time, and was trying to snuggle up to his mother for warmth. But she was gradually growing colder and colder in the icy blast from the snow on Rhewyn. He called, in vain, for his mother to turn her head towards him to warm him with her breath, and give him succour. But she was getting colder all the time. Bringing her lamb into the world in the cold, in a lonely corner of the Cae Mawr, had proved too much for her, and the feeble cry rent the air without a soul to hear it except the owl, who bent its head to listen for any footsteps in the vicinity before venturing to the Cae Mawr and the lamb, who was vainly trying to nestle up to his mother's wool for warmth. The owl is the first to notice the cry of a sickly, lonely lamb. But although it is a very weak cry, it is one that the farmer, too, hears from afar, and before long a tall man could be seen cutting his way through a hedge in the distance, and making his way across Cae Mawr towards the lamb. Night had fallen by now, but the moon was beginning to shine, and the land was light again. The man lit a lantern he had with him, and you could see from its light that he was the Master of Pen y Bryn. He comforted the lamb and put the mother carefully under the shade of a branch, with the instinctive tenderness of a man towards the dead — as if the hoar-frost could cause her suffering. He went back to the lamb, took it in the crook of his arm, and sheltered it in his breast; then he went through the gate, closed it carefully, put his lantern down on the other side, rested his elbow on the gate and stopped there to look around him at the farm that had reclaimed his soul for some time by now. A merciful crust had formed over the wound which his ego had suffered when his horse fell, with its load of coal, at the beginning of winter; by now the story was old hat and everyone had forgotten it.

He did not see David Hughes the carpenter for days after asking his advice about leaving the farm, and he was a person who had to function in the heat of passion, or not function at all. And when David Hughes had finished thinking out his reply, the Master of Pen y Bryn was seeing things more clearly, and took every opportunity of avoiding him. It was now five months since the day he asked for that advice, and still David Hughes had had no opprtunity to express an opinion. And tonight the Master of Pen y Bryn was leaning on the Cae Mawr gate, looking over his farm, with a little lamb clasped to his breast and a lantern at his feet. The lamb bleated softly and contentedly, and his own mind wandered to the ewe mother who lay dead under the tree, and from her to several other dead mothers he had lost this season. He went from meadow to meadow in his mind, recollecting all the circumstances of his life in conjunction with them, many times over; and after each expedition he always ended up beside the dead mother of the little lamb he now had in his arms. All this made him feel rather depressed; and he asked himself why he had to suffer all these losses. Then he began to count his virtues, and he saw that they were many. His mind wandered again from meadow to meadow, and from dead mother to dead mother, and back to the dead mother of the lamb he was holding. For a bit of diversion, he counted his virtues again, and again saw that they were many. Suddenly he heard a light rustle at his side, a bird rustling its wing in sleep. Then something else rustling, which the bird's wing had woken up — the rustle of a rabbit in the dead leaves which, for some reason, it had chosen for its night's shelter instead of its warren. He thought about these movements, and he felt jealous of the world of the bird and the rabbit. At that moment came the clear, precise to-who of an owl over the land, and within a second the baying of a fox somewhere in the depths of the forest. But the sounds conveyed nothing to him; he was so obsessed with his own troubles. He did not notice that the bird had stopped rustling its wings and the rabbit had stopped scuffling in the leaves. Gradually, the Master's soul grew embittered. He felt like picking a quarrel with the world and everyone and everything, and even with the divine order; and he went over his own numerous virtues for the third time.

He was beginning to feel the cold biting, and hewent down to pick up the lantern to go home; but then the sound of clumsy footsteps came shambling up the road, and since the traveller would have to pass him he decided to wait and see who it was, and left his lantern on the ground. It was old Mally Francis, with a quart tin in her hand; when he saw her the Master of Pen y Bryn knew what her errand was — she was going to Pen y Bryn to beg a bit of dripping for her children. Mally Francis was very solicitous about her children, though they were all ashamed of her. She was one of the world's unfortunates; her fate was like that of the occasional chieftain one hears about in barbaric countries who is granted the royal prerogative for the time being, on condition that he allows his flatterers to trample him underfoot some time later in deference to their gods. Mally had three or four children, but she had never been married, and she took care of the children of her shame as best she could by begging, and doing an occasional casual day's work. She was not old — about the same age as the man leaning on the gate waiting for her — but she looked old, because society, after dethroning her, had trampled her underfoot. Now she was just the object of the mockery of children, the scorn of the pretentious and the contempt of respectable people. And the Master of Pen y Bryn put himself in the third category.

He waited for her with contempt in his gaze. When she came up to him he said: "Well, Mally, where are you off to now?" Mally stopped and curtseyed nervously to him, and said *sotto voce*: "I'm off to Pen y Bryn, sir, to see if Mrs. Williams has got a bit of dripping." She curtseyed again and dragged herself clumsily on; and the Master of Pen y Bryn noticed, in the light of the lantern, that as she passed she had trampled on an early daisy which was growing on some turf at the side of the road; but he thought nothing of it at the time. He thought of Mally and her way of life. With a touch of malice — malice which he would not have wanted his comrades on life's journey to see — he recalled the career of Mally Francis. He remembered the time when she was not "old Mally Francis"; she was Mary Georgina Francis, or Miss Francis, then, a graceful, attractive girl who was courted by the best lads in the neighbourhood. At that time, he had a vague feeling that she was above him; in view of that recollection the memory of the deep curtsey of a moment ago was rather gratifying. He remembered the rumour that circulated amongst the lads in the village, started by some starched-up dandy who should know, that indefinable rumour, that Miss Francis was rather a loose young lady. It was then that he ventured to go out with her.

When he thought of those occasions, the Master of Pen y Bryn began to mutter to himself. "So that is how it is with Mary Georgina Francis?" he said slowly and with emphasis. He began to smile when he remembered one refusal he got from her, when he once offered to take her for a walk before the dandy got hold of her, and before the rumour spread amongst the local lads. He wiped his feet forcefully in the green grass, but it was Mally Francis, not the grass, that he envisaged as the carpet. The smile stayed longer on his face than he cared to admit next morning, but suddenly it gave way to a pallor like the pallor of death. He thought he heard a clear, categorical voice from somewhere in the darkness, asking how much he had contributed to her downfall. The Master of Pen y Bryn did a strange thing when he heard the voice; he bent down and put out the lantern. But in spite of putting out the lantern and closing his eyes twice, three times, he could not help seeing Mally Francis clearly before him, just as she used to be, in her former beauty. Very slowly, the vision grew dimmer, and as it dimmed it became more like Mally Francis as he had seen her a few moments ago — covered in mud and dirt from top to toe. When the vision had faded he raised his hand, and rubbed his own breast in the region of his heart, quite subconsciously, as if he were rubbing dirt away. He went on rubbing his breast for some time, looking into the night where the ghost had vanished. He listened, holding his breath, for the strange voice again, but he heard nothing but the contented bleating of the innocent lamb that looked deep into his eyes.

Soon, he caught himself walking towards home after Mally Francis, hiding behind branches and mounds, but quite unable to shift his gaze from the direction in which she had gone. He was within a stone's throw of her when she got to the house. He could see his wife opening the door, and Mally curtseying to her, and telling her tale. He felt a certain amount of pride when he saw the difference between them, and the curtsey. But another vision flashed before his eyes which made him hide his face; in this one, he could see his wife standing by his side at the altar of God, an altar which Mally had never reached, and had never defiled. His wife's wedding dress and his own person were covered with the same dirt as he had seen in the vision by the Cae Mawr gate, all over Mally. The Master of Pen y Bryn moaned, and he stayed beneath the shelter of a branch to stare at Mally by the door, toadying to his wife, and curtseying for the dripping. He moaned again, thinking of that curtsey.

The innocent little lamb bleated again, contented, and its bearer was very frightened, because he thought the clear voice was coming back; he forgot that he was holding the lamb to his breast although his arm had become quite numb in the process. He remembered his lantern, and went back without thinking of removing the lamb from his breast. On the contrary; he pressed it to him as if that helped to thrust innocence into his heart. He went back for the lantern and lit it; put the lamb down carefully, and started to search; and he went on searching till he heard Mally's voice again, inquiring: "Lost something, Mr. Williams?" She curtseyed to him and vanished awkwardly into the night. He was searching, half-bemused, for the daisy he had seen her trample on. He found it and went on his knees. He lifted it up, put soil all around it, and drew his hand tenderly over its leaves and petals to smooth it, till it looked like a flower that was growing normally again. He did not know why he did this, but the action soothed the agony in the depths of his heart, and he felt, in a muddled vague sort of way that his attempt to put the little flower to rights and helping it to grow again was a kind of reparation for something he was not at all clear about in his mind. But the Master did not notice that the daisy had been broken down to its root; and then he got up and thought of another flower that had been broken at the root — Mally Francis.

Mally curtseyed to him on the way to Pen y Bryn, and he felt he had deserved it; but as for the curtsey on the way back — it was as if someone had heaped coals of fire on his head. He started to analyse, leaning on the gate again with the lamb at his breast. Why, he asked, did she curtsey to him? Did she still remember the way he made advances to her once? Did she recall her own former status? If so, why did she curtsey to him? Why did all the lower classes bow and scrape to him? Did the curtsey of the rest mean the same as her curtsey? She could hardly feel respect for him when she had been contaminated by him. Were the vagaries of his youth forgotten in the neighbourhood? If not, why did he hear nothing of them? Whatever respect she might feel for the Master of Pen y Bryn, then, she could not think much of John Williams. True, the undercurrent of scorn which the neighbourhood had always felt for him had never come to the surface; but it was equally true that he had never trodden on the corns of the working classes, and the working class has a long memory when you tread on its corns. A great passionate yearning swept over him — to be able to shake himself free from the world of Mally Francis and her kind, and to eliminate a lifetime of weaknesses and peccadilloes from the local consciousness. He knew there was only one way to do it — to perform some great, romantic, glorious deed, to inspire enthusiasm and ecstasy which would consume the past like a bonfire. But he did not know what great, romantic, glorious deed he could perform.

At this moment he heard footsteps coming up the road, and as the travellers approached he recognised them — David Hughes, the carpenter, and Mr. Roberts, the minister. Or, to give him his name as it always appeared in print, the Rev. T. Cefnllech Roberts. They were coming to Pen y Bryn for a chat. "So what are you doing here?" asked David Hughes when he came to the gate. Whereupon the lamb grew restless and bleated merrily.

"A little lamb!" said the minister. "How are you, John Williams?"

The Master of Pen y Bryn replied that he was quite well. David Hughes had noticed by now that he looked very odd, and his hopes for a chance to give his advice sank; for the

Master of Pen y Bryn looked like someone gazing at a ghost. The bleating of the lamb roused its protector; he pulled himself together and tried to look natural. He told the story of the dead mother and how he succoured the lamb, and the three of them made for the house. He chatted for a moment and then fell silent again, and he would find himself dwelling on Mally Francis, and trying to solve the riddle of her curtsey, and he felt he had never sunk so low in local opinion as now. Then he remembered that he was supposed to look natural, and he asked Mr. Roberts, the minister for the latest news.

"News?" said Mr. Roberts enthusiastically, "great news! Wales is awakening, her night is fading, and she is beginning to cast off the yoke of centuries." The minister was in his element now. No matter whether he himself was heroic or not, he never tired of praising the heroism of Wales, and he trotted out his stock of available clichés on demand. He talked of the dawn breaking, and shackles being cast aside, and the yoke of oppression being broken; the mountains bursting into song, and the trees clapping hands for joy in sheer anticipation. He treated the Master of Pen y Bryn to a mass of verbiage before he even told him the news. The other knew that there was something unusual afoot, and he held his breath. When Mr. Roberts had finished his introduction and pitched his voice ready for a fiery sermon, he said that the tithe war had reached the parish boundary and that Frank Bryan, Y Bryniau, and John Jones, Rhos Uchaf, had decided not to pay it; the countryside was in a turmoil and everyone practically worshipped them. He asked the Master of Pen y Bryn.what he thought of all this, but the latter had sunk into his shell, and did not reply. David Hughes and the minister conducted an awkward conversation to wait for the Master of Pen y Bryn to get into a communicative mood. His mind was wandering to Mally Francis and his early days, and him and his wife before the altar of God with slime on their clothes, and how the local people remembered all this. He did not think beyond this. He felt vaguely that he could see the locals smirking behind his back after curtseying to his face, and his whole soul revolted. He remembered the minister saying that the people half worshipped Frank Bryan and John Jones; he turned to him and said, slowly and with emotion:

"Mr. Roberts, I don't want to pay the tithe either." David Hughes sniggered when he heard this, but Mr. Roberts resumed, with doubled enthusiasm, his oration about how the dawn was breaking, and shackles were being cast away, and the yoke of centuries of oppression was being broken, the mountains bursting into song and the trees applauding; and this time he added that the flowers would dance and the animals would leap at the sight of Wales awakening.

They entered Pen y Bryn, the three of them. John Williams could not look his wife in the eye when he went in, and he blamed the sudden glare of the lamplight. David Hughes did not say much; he was pondering on the meaning of the Master's decision not to pay the tithe. He did not want to persuade him to break his promise; he consoled himself with the thought that the Master of Pen y Bryn was not as perspicacious as he himself was. As for Mr. Roberts the minister, his eloquence knew no limits. Everything was wonderful to him that evening — Wales awakening, and the coming of the millennium. Poor fellow.

"Mr. Roberts," said Jane Williams, interrupting his speech rather patronisingly, "we killed a pig earlier this week; would you like a piece of pork to take home to Mrs. Roberts?"

Mr. Roberts thanked her for it, and fell silent. He knew very well that the giving and receiving of the pork was a sign that Wales was not yet awake, for it was offered to the minister, not the carpenter, and Jane Williams would not dream of offering it to the carpenter. But it is difficult to refuse when you have a wife and five children to support, and you are finding it hard to make ends meet. No, Wales had not woken up yet; so Mr. Roberts, the minister, took the pork home with a clear conscience. Or at least, he started out with one.

Chapter VI

The Rev. T. Cefnllech Roberts started out from Pen y Bryn with a clear conscience and the hunk of pork under his arm, accompanied by David Hughes the carpenter. His secret desire at that moment to convince himself that Wales had *not* woken up was so strong that he forgot to talk to David Hughes for part of the way. He found it pleasant to think that Wales had not woken up, because having to live on charity does not seem as repulsive by night as it does by day; you lose sight of it in the general blackness. No doubt his conscience would have remained dormant that night, at least, if David Hughes had not hinted that he felt just the same way about the gift as the minister did.

"Those people at Pen y Bryn are terribly kind," said David Hughes; "Mr. Williams' father was very kind, especially to ministers. No one was ever more indebted to anybody than the ministers were to old Mr. Williams."

"So I've often heard," said the minister; "but I never had the pleasure of knowing him."

"Yes," said the carpenter, "and he felt it very badly when the old William Williams threatened to ban the present Mr. Williams publicly from the fellowship meeting, when he got married; and no one had ever been as kind to William Williams as the old gentleman from Pen y Bryn." But there was a strange bitterness underlying the urbane sympathy in David Hughes' voice.

"Which William Williams was that then?" asked the minister, again feeling grateful that it was dark, because conscience, which was beginning to shuffle uneasily in its slumber, was making the blood rush to his cheeks. Had not he, too, fallen into the trap of kindness? If it had not been night, David Hughes would have seen him blush; but apart from that, the minister would have seen a half-mischievous, half-malicious gleam in the carpenter's eyes — which would have made his motive for stressing the Pen y Bryn family's kindness to ministers quite obvious.

"We used to call him William Williams (Ch)," said David Hughes, "because he couldn't say 'r' properly. His 'r' was a kind of semi-ch. He was a brusque sort of man, who never remembered kindnesses, but he always claimed to be bound by conscience. He was the only man of that kind I ever remember here; most of the ones that followed were nice, kind fellows, and the present Mr. Williams, like his father, was very decent to them all. And he still is, as you noticed tonight."

They said goodbye at the minister's house. The minister gave his wife the piece of pork, and she was so overjoyed that she cried her heart out. Her husband went to his room and closed the door. He did not light the lamp or light the fire. It was quite light and warm enough for what he had in mind. He laid his arms on the table, and his head on his arms, and sighed like a man without hope. He did not know where to run to from the souls of the thousand visions he had murdered; those whom he once loved and whose company he delighted in.

These visions had been his friends and his main source of joy. They were his companions at every turn; he and they knew of every shady nook and path in his old neighbourhood, and no hour was too late to be with them. But he had murdered them one by one; and now their spirits were persecuting him, staring satanically at him in the night; the fear and trembling they aroused in him were frightful. And there he was, his head resting on his arms on the table, trying to blot out the sight of them, but they came despite all that, their warmest welcome a malicious smirk. He recollected, as he gazed on them in turn, how he had cherished them once, what bliss it had been to be with them; for he had longed for the day's work to end so that he could go back to them. He used to meet them in the neighbourhood's sequestered glades, with the eagerness of a lover meeting the girl with whom he was destined to share his life. They would come, one after the other, in all their glory. But then came the night, and treason, and murder, and the angels turned to fiends to torment him in the darkest nights of his soul. And this hour was one of the darkest.

The Rev. T. Cefnllech Roberts was one of life's tragic souls. When he was born, Welsh life was full of romance; Wales was awakening to the dawn of her youth, and its light shone on her face. Ministers of the gospel had long fought her battles, till they became heroes in her eyes, bathed in a supernatural aura. At that time, offerings were cast at their feet like the palms at the feet of their Master, and there was great rejoicing when one of them came on a passing visit to the country districts. Many lads were dazzled by this charisma, and longed to enter their world. One of these lads was the one who later became the Rev. T. Cefnllech Roberts. By the time he had joined their ranks the glory had vanished; the minister's glamour had become an actor's royal regalia in the hard light of day.

His parents had never had the honour of giving a minister a night's lodging, and their relationship with him was that of people who gazed at a monarch from afar. They never dared imagine that one of their children could become a minister, but their cup would be overflowing if this should happen. They could not conceive of greater bliss. They respected ministers so much that even a slip of a lad, a lay preacher on trial, would get endless adulation from them when he dropped in for a bite. In return they would get the honour of feeding a lay preacher on trial. This was the atmosphere the Rev. T. Cefnllech Roberts was brought up in, and faith in preachers was kindled in him early; and faith in his country, which seemed to blossom under their ministry. And his ideal was to be a Welsh minister, preaching the eternal gospel in a musical burst of Welsh hwyl, and proclaiming the rights of his country amid enthusiasm and hand-clapping and feet-stamping. He tried out his talents a great deal on many congregations of stones and many flocks of sheep on the mountain. In this way he became acquainted, early in his career, with two rather unpleasant types of audience — the immovable and the mindless. The stones gazed stoically and contemptuously at him, and the sheep looked bewildered, as if they could not understand a word.

When he began to preach his soul was on fire, and like every young preacher he thought that before long he could inspire the land with ardour for the pure and the elevated, and that multitudes would throng to the Saviour under his ministry. He mercilessly condemned all manner of sin, thinking that he would only have to condemn and the land would awaken, be afraid, and become converted. It was then he learnt the phrases that became a part of him: that the dawn was rising in Wales, shackles were being cast away, the yoke of oppression was being broken, the mountains were bursting into song, the trees were applauding for joy — in anticipation of this event.

It was to Llanalun that he first went as a minister. In Llanalun, at the begining of autumn, they had a fair they called Dung Fair — an ancient institution. In the first half of the day they had an animal market and in the second they had fun. People would then indulge frantically in play and dance and drunkenness and fighting. The minister imagined devils sniggering and angels weeping when the fun and games were over — when he watched the horde of wayfarers staggering home, and among them an occasional couple who would not get home at all that night.

The Rev. T. Cefnllech Roberts, with the curiosity of a new minister, went to investigate the fair, and he was shocked to the core. He left the place with all the visions of his youth hovering around him, calling him to action; their voices were like a cry from the promised land. And he decided to act, to banish such vanity from the land. The next day he went to his fellow ministers in the area, old men who had lived there a long time. One of them intimated to him, kindly, that it was a great thing to be young, and the other hinted to him just as kindly that the fair had been in Llanalun before his time, and that in all probability it would be there after him, and all that went with it. He stared at them with the astonishment of a child let down by his father, and he saw that the diamonds in the crowns he had once admired so much were just paste.

Then he went to the local church deacons. They, too, were very sympathetic, but hinted that his older brothers in the ministry had earned their good name by keeping quiet. He, too, would see that it was best to keep his mouth shut, if he stopped to think; it was always an excellent thing to be circumspect. Dung Fair only came once a year and there was a year of potential repentance between each one. The Rev. T. Cefnllech Roberts went home to think, but his visions would not let him think. They surrounded him, a swarming mass, with deafening cries. In the end he caught one of them, the one that cried the loudest, and killed it then and there; he gave it as a peace offering to the neighbourhood, and so saved his good name. When he had killed that one, the others fled over the distant hills like a frightened flock of birds. The silence that followed was so oppressive that he wished them back, screams and all, and he went on wishing till he lured them back again; all except the one he had killed. But the death of the one had brought a certain sadness to the voices and eyes of the others, till life became a burden to him on those occasions when he saw and heard them.

He felt sometimes that he was out of his depth. He had neither the courage nor the genius to overcome, so he always had to make a peace offering; and in that offering his visions vanished one by one. He discovered, gradually, that his *forte* did not lie in his preaching, or in his courage either, and he was in this state when he came to Llangeunant. There, he would have opportunities for a fresh start — but he very soon found that he could not start afresh in his new surroundings; he could only pick up where he had left off before. The murdered visions would not come back. Llangeunant was a very hospitable place, and the locals were perpetually giving him the produce of the land as gifts; but he could see that this was not his utopia either. He was called upon, from time to time, to act according to his conscience, but some gift or tutelage stood perpetually in his way, and he could not retreat to the company of his spiritual visions for help and comfort, for he had sacrificed them all, one by one, on the altar of peace and quiet. He had no companionship now but the local people, for the murderer of visions cannot resurrect them, though he destroy himself in the process.

The Rev. T. Cefnllech Roberts saw that much of the respect for ministers which prevailed in his young day persisted in Llangeunant, and that every visit he made to his flock was appreciated. He began to make a point of visiting. He went to their houses and took an interest in their work. He went to the ploughmen in the fields and took hold of the handles of the plough, and for days afterwards they talked about how Mr. Roberts the minister tried to plough in such and such a field, and recalled every gesture and remark he made in the attempt. He talked to farmers about their animals and took an interest in their crops. He visited the fairs, and everyone felt honoured by his presence.

A typical conversation at a fair went like this:

"What'll you take for the cow, William Edwards? Good fellowship meeting last night, wasn't it?"

"Twelve pounds, Hugh Roberts. Didn't old Peter Hughes make a wonderful speech?"

"Too much by half, William Edwards. Yes, old Peter was good. But here comes Mr. Roberts the minister. Nice man, Mr. Roberts."

Whereupon Mr. Roberts would pass by and pretend to bargain with them. Then he would go to others and do the same thing — smile and joke and play at bargaining, and William Edwards and Hugh Roberts felt greatly honoured. They were so taken with Mr. Roberts' feeble banter that they would forget the cow for a bit. They would say how they respected him, repeating some hoary old jokes he had cracked at the last fair; and each one would make a secret resolve in his own mind to send him something from his produce when he got home. This is what most people did eventually, when Mr. Roberts had been cracking jokes with them. And their word for him was one which, in his best moments, he thoroughly detested: he was a nice man. To him, the most degrading depth a minister could sink to was to be called a nice man. Even so, he could not help knowing that he, himself, was rapidly degenerating into a nice man.

When he got married, he noticed another sign of his country's respect for her ministers — she respected them too much to dare suggest that they were mercenary enough to want a living wage. Did they not exist solely for the Gospel? This experience was made all the more bitter by the people's obvious expectations of him, and the ideas they obviously had about his so-called means. As his family increased, his courage diminished, and he came to accept gratefully gifts which would have stuck in his gullet at the beginning of his career, because he feared he might become dependent on them. Poor man; he not only sacrificed his visions, he gradually sacrificed his heart's blood for his family and his fellow sufferers. He was forced to endure the greatest curse of all time — the curse of earning his crust by being a nice man.

Yes, the Rev. T. Cefnllech Roberts was one of the world's tragic souls, one who found his own life a disappointment, and who discovered, when he had grown too old to change, that he was not cut out to suffer the agony which prophets are accustomed to bear. His tragedy was doubled by his own servile demeanour, which earned him great respect in his parish.

While the Rev. T. Cefnllech Roberts was sitting in his room like this, the Master of Pen y Bryn was sitting at home with his legs crossed, looking into the fire; the expression on his face was as heroic as he could afford, seeing that he had lived for such a short time in the world of heroes. Jane Williams was standing in the middle of the floor, her spectacles on her nose and her thumb on her lips; she looked at her husband over her glasses, startled and admiring. As her admiration grew she would change a thumb for a finger and a finger for a thumb. Sometimes a shadow of doubt crossed her face, as if she were not sure whether her husband's action was the wisest possible; and then she would throw her head back and look at him *through* her spectacles. She pursed her lips and put her hand down, then lifted it again; she put her thumb on her lips again and looked admiringly at her husband over her spectacles, as if the question of his sagacity had been settled once and for all in his favour. Only one thing troubled her: that David Hughes had not congratulated him. Her husband knew he was being subjected to this scrutiny, and tried to accentuate the heroic expression on his face, but slowly, so that the change would not be too obvious; for he wanted to give the impression that this action was just his innate character blossoming forth.

"John," said Jane Williams in a while.

"What?" said John Williams.

"So you're not going to pay the tithe — well, what will Mr. Jones the parson say?" she asked.

"What does it matter to me what he says?" asked John Williams defiantly.

"Of course," said Jane Williams: "After all, who is Mr. Jones the parson?"

She bit her lip as she said this, just a very little, thinking that she was one of the fortunate élite on whom Mrs. Jones bestowed a smile and a handshake, but the defiant look on her husband's face was enough to make up for that. Jane Williams licked her lips as if she were ashamed of the tiny little bite and wanted to eliminate the traces. A long silence fell again.

"John," said Jane Williams in a while.

"Well?" asked John Williams, patronisingly.

"I've been thinking," said Jane.

"Oh," John Williams said, rubbing his eyes.

"Yes," said Jane, falling silent again, and looking eagerly over her glasses with her thumb on her lip.

After she had been silent for as long as she considered proper, Jane Williams called her husband's name again, and John Williams said "What?" again.

"Well," said Jane, "what I'm saying is, I've been thinking." She stressed the last word.

"Thinking about what?" asked John unbelievingly.

"Thinking," said Jane, drawing herself up, "that the neighbourhood should know what sort of man they have living in their midst." A stranger listening to this would have got the impression that the Master of Pen y Bryn was the only *man* in the locality.

"It'll get to know soon enough," said John Williams.

"But it ought to have the honour of seeing and hearing the man," said Jane.

John Williams realised then that his wife had, indeed, been thinking and he bent his head inquiringly.

"Yes," said his wife, as if her mental feat were the most natural thing on earth. After a meditative silence: "It would be a good thing if you were to chair a concert," she said.

"Chair a concert?" asked John Williams, surprised.

"Yes, and you could make a speech to say why you won't pay the tithe, and you'd get deafening applause. And you deserve it too," said Jane Williams, closing her lips as if the last word ever had passed them, and she would be willing to die after this tribute to her spouse's worth.

The suggestion appealed to John Williams; he forgot that the attributes of a hero are that he does not shout, or raise himself up, or let his voice be heard on the highway. But he knew of no concert he could be chairman of, and he knew of no one who would be willing to put him up for chairman if there had been one. For up to now no one had seen fit to put him up for chairman of any meeting, so he looked dubious and fell silent. This was his wife's cue to chip in again.

"Bethania Eisteddfod will be held in a month," she said. To her, an eisteddfod and a competitive meeting and a concert were all the same thing.

"Yes," said John Williams.

"Why can't you be chairman of that?" asked Jane Williams. "They were announcing the committee meeting for the day after tomorrow."

She raised her voice and drew herself up as she spoke, as if she were defying the whole universe.

John Williams did not know, either, why he could not be chairman of that, and he looked entreatingly at his wife. She asked him the question again, more confidingly, and John replied that he did not know, though he admitted freely, between him and his wife, that his not paying the tithe should make a favourable impression on the neighbourhood. But since he was so unaccustomed to being chairman, what if no one thought of putting him forward?

"I've got the very man," said Jane Williams, seeing that her husband was receptive to the suggestion.

"Who's that?"

"Mr. Roberts the minister," said Jane Williams *sotto voce.*

John Williams' face lit up, but at the same time he asked if it would be right and proper to ask Mr. Roberts.

"Well," said Jane Williams, "he looked very glad of that pork tonight." And the two of them smiled, like people who have understood each other for years. "Now let's strike while the iron is hot," said Jane.

"Strike — what d'you mean?" her husband asked.

"Let's go now to Mr. Roberts," said Jane Williams, "and ask him. It's not ten o'clock yet, and he stays in his study very late, they say."

The pair set out without uttering another word. Jane Williams put a basket with some eggs in it under her cloak, and off they went. It was a fine night, with the moon floating on the air, and John Williams, in the moonlight, felt the full effect of the romantic heroism that encircled them. They got to the minister's house. When they were about to knock the minister was standing in his room; he had got up and made up his mind for good and all that he was going to embark on a new phase of his existence. He looked at each of the four walls of his room in turn, and raised his fist towards them as if he wanted to defy the four winds of heaven, and he emphasized every gesture of defiance by stamping his heel heavily on the floor. His wife was getting the children ready for bed, and they were all in a gay mood in anticipation of tomorrow's dinner. There was a knock on the door, and when they opened it, Mr. and Mrs. Williams,

Pen y Bryn, came in, and received a royal welcome. Mrs. Roberts felt the world was much too kind to her when she got the eggs, and she said so over and over again to her husband and to Mr. and Mrs. Williams, and to each individual egg as she pulled it out of the basket.

They talked about trivialities, loudly and clearly, for a while, then they all began to talk in whispers, and Jane Williams was the chief whisperer. The minister smiled and listened and listened and smiled. Soon Mr. and Mrs. Williams got up to go home, and Mr. and Mrs. Roberts saw them to the door, smiling and talking and talking and smiling, and Mr. Roberts assured them that everything would be all right, that they should not worry at all — he would fix everything. Everyone said an affectionate good night, and off went the Master and Mistress of Pen y Bryn. Mrs. Roberts hurried to the kitchen and the children, but her husband, when he had shut the door, stayed in the hall, key in hand, and the key stayed in his hand heaven knows how long. Mrs. Roberts got the children off to bed, but he stayed where he was. She came to him to tell him gently (for Mrs. Roberts knew her husband) that the purpose of a key, at that time of night, was to lock a door. He locked it obediently and went to the fire in the kitchen. He sat down and gazed for ages at nothing. He had a vision of heaven before his eyes, peopled by his stronger Welsh brothers who had been able to defy, successfully, the great damnation to which he had had to succumb.

Chapter VII

The tumult of the tithe war came to Llangeunant and the surrounding area like a sweeping tide. At first, it was a kind of strange murmur in the distance, which no one could understand — the subject of mockery, and anxiety, and boastfulness, and fear. Then came a wave; it broke on the shore of the local way of life, and receded again, it brought with it a pleasant, restless thrill. Before long a stronger wave came, with an increasing dread in its wake, and all the more pleasant for that; and it, too, receded. Then, yet another wave, stronger still, shattering the toys and sandcastles which many people had built, through a childlike faith in those who wielded authority and patronage in the neighbourhood. Finally, the big wave came, casting everyone into the depths to fight for dear life. Its force was so incredible that you could see but few heads above water. The others, in madness and despair, plumbed the dark ocean of tyranny and oppression.

Llangeunant was not used to such a tempest. Some preacher had told the people in a sermon that the sea was beginning to heave, and its waves to roar, referring to the war that lay in store for them; but not many of them had seen the sea. For them, the sea belonged to a land of dreams and poetry and romance. They had a popular hymn which ran:

"Ar fôr tymhestlog teithio'r wyf i fyd sydd well i fyw,
Gan wenu ar ei stormydd oll — fy Nhad sydd wrth y llyw."

("I am voyaging on a stormy sea, to a fairer land to live in,

And I smile in the face of all tempests; my Father is at the helm").

And most of them nurtured a vague, nebulous feeling that the sea was something to smile upon.

The light murmur of a distant war had its allure, and the allure grew as its sound increased. But the attraction vanished when the big wave came. Then, when the danger was over, the glamour came back.

Frank Bryan, Y Bryniau, John Jones, Y Rhos Uchaf, Samuel Jones, Y Tŷ Glas, and the Master of Pen y Bryn were among the few who kept their heads above water. A lot of people expected David Hughes, the carpenter, to be among them, but he was not, and most people made excuses for him because he had advocated keeping the law for quite a long time before the matter of breaking it came up. But there were some who regarded him differently from the rest of the populace; even he did not escape unscathed.

There was a narrow, dark, tree-lined road between Llangeunant and the village of Pandy, and a house on the road, about a mile from the village, called Tu Hwnt i'r Afon. Richard Davies, the cleaner at Bethania Chapel, his wife, and Mary his daughter lived there. Like the rest of the young people, Mary had a very high regard for David Hughes the carpenter. From Tu Hwnt i'r Afon, in the silence of night, you could hear footsteps on the road from a considerable distance. Mary used to like sitting on her bed, leaning on her window sill, looking out at the world, and listening late into the night — or what country people regard as late. One evening she sat up very late, half dreaming; it was a quiet, oppressive night, dark as pitch. She heard footsteps approaching, slowly and deliberately, from a distance. Then, other footsteps could be heard from the opposite direction, just as slow and deliberate. She listened to them, in that suffocating silence, for a long time as they approached each other. She gathered from the cough of one of the persons that it was David Hughes the carpenter, but she could not make the other out. Eventually they met, almost immediately beneath her window, and halted. Neither moved, and neither spoke, for a while. The silence, in the expectant throb of the air, was palpable.

David Hughes was the first to break the silence. He asked uneasily: "Well, how are you this evening?" No answer for a moment, then Mary heard a brusque, deep voice, that she knew well, whispering slowly and scathingly: "Traitor." They both stood silent again, as quiet and still as if they had not been there at all. Then each went on his own way without saying another word, and Mary listened, bewildered, to the sound of their feet slowly vanishing in the distance; one sound was lighter, more awkward, the other steady and heavy. Soon they were completely lost in the night.

It was the Master of Pen y Bryn that was most talked about. He was the talk of the shops, the workrooms, the highway and the taverns. The others' refusal to pay was discussed just as you might say that two and two make four; you would expect nothing else. As for the Master of Pen y Bryn, everyone talked about him as if someone had found a way of making two and two into five, and everyone wanted to be first with the news; the news which transformed all their attitudes and reshaped their lives.

These four and their like had been united in the anti-tithe movement, so it would be natural to think that they were all in harmony with their group. But heroes and their wives are human, after all. It was Margaret Jones, Y Tŷ Glas, Samuel Jones' wife, who seemed most upset about the way people were talking. Frank Bryan was a widower; his daughter kept house for him, and the mistress of Y Rhos Uchaf was a harmless, quiet sort of woman. But the mistress of Tŷ Glas felt she had enough personality to put the whole neighbourhood in its place, and she decided that it was her duty to do so, whatever her husband might think. Not paying the tithe when the call came meant nothing more to him than going out milking when he heard the cows lowing in the yard, or feeding the pigs when they squealed — it was just duty. But Margaret Jones thought differently. She was determined to propagate her beliefs, come what may, resorting to persecution if need be; and her acts of persecution sometimes preceded the propaganda.

Margaret Jones, Y Tŷ Glas, was a woman worth knowing. She was a tall, broad female, with auburn hair and big black eyes. She always spoke as if she had a head cold, or as if she were trying to reveal a secret to her neighbour in an inquisitive congregation. When she and her husband conversed by the fire, their voices had that sound you get sometimes from a mildewed organ — the lower note sticking and vibrating and the air escaping half audibly from the bellows at the same time. Margaret Jones walked differently from most, too. Imagine someone with raw flesh on his soles and a healthy pair of heels — this was how Margaret Jones walked. The nearest thing to this is a cat walking on embers, which was how Margaret Jones walked, so that often she was at your side before you knew it. She could see the funny side of every story she told.She began every story, and every other form of conversation for that matter, in the same way. She would laugh, and look past the person she was speaking to, into the distance, as if she could see the jokes approaching over the horizon. The only difference in the way she started various conversations was in the degree and duration of the laughter, which ranged from a brief clucking to a great hearty yell.

When she prepared food for whoever happened to be visiting her, Margaret Jones would go and cut some bread, and when she had cut two inches or so she would remove the knife from the loaf, put it on the table and start laughing. Everyone within reach would smile out of politeness and anticipation. Margaret Jones would tell her story and take up the knife again; then she would pull it another two inches or so through the loaf, put it down again, and start laughing afresh. This time she might come and tell the story in your ear, and then go back to finish cutting the slice of bread. She did the rest of the work in instalments, from taking the kettle off the fire, putting tea in the pot and pouring water into it, to pouring it into the cups.

This, then, was the woman who opposed the Master of Pen y Bryn's *new* status in the district. When the tithe war came and everybody started talking about the Master of Pen y Bryn, she set to, in her own way, to show how silly it was to talk about him and his heroism when there were other men as good as he around. This is how Margaret Jones spread her message. She would start laughing in mid-conversation, and having got her companion smiling equably, she would trot out the phrase: "The Master of Pen y Bryn", and then break into another fit of laughter. Her companion would join in out of politeness, pretending that the Master's very name was a first-class joke. Seeing the other laughing, Margaret Jones for her part would laugh more uproariously than ever, till the wave reached its peak and started flowing back. Then she would say under her breath that there was nothing more wonderful in the Master of Pen y Bryn not paying the tithe than anybody else like him; it was just a stupid story. Then she would lower her voice into a whisper, and apply to the story the description "silly shivlings". And these two words just about summed up the secret.

Margaret Jones had her own hotchpotch of verbiage, and it was quite out of the ordinary. Everything was either shivlings or solid. If she talked about breaking a dish, she would start as usual by laughing to herself, then she would say that the dish shattered into fragments; she would lower her voice, emphasising the secrecy of the question, bend her head forward and add quietly, "shattered to shivlings." If Margaret Jones told you how long she worked on washday, she would say that she had been doing the washing for three hours, more or less; then she would lower her voice and add in a whisper, "three hours solid." Her listeners always appreciated these public confidences.

Margaret Jones felt that Mrs. Jones, Y Rhos Uchaf, would be the audience most likely to sympathize with the truth of her sermon in these particular circumstances. Mrs. Jones listened to her, smiling pleasantly, like someone enjoying a service, but she did not shout "Amen" because she wanted to stay friendly with Mrs. Williams, Pen y Bryn.

And as the murmur of war grew louder, these ladies were seen in Llangeunant more often than usual. Mrs. Jones, Y Rhos Uchaf, would go about her business hurriedly and shy-looking, and scurry off again. At first her husband used to follow her in a carriage, but when people mustered up the courage to come out on their doorsteps and shout "hurrah", he stopped going, and Mrs. Jones, too, had to curtail her visits out of embarrassment.

As for Mrs. Williams, Pen y Bryn, she used to walk down to the village with a self-possessed, dignified air, looking over her spectacles, her eye always on her destination; but the journey grew longer in proportion to the applause.

Margaret Jones (no one ever called her anything else) would stop and chat with everyone she met, enlightening them as to the comparative virtues of her spouse and the Master of Pen y Bryn. Mrs. Jane Williams would do the same in her own special way.

It was not only Margaret Jones, however, who was affected by the rumpus. It was like electricity in the air, and it galvanized everybody. The school children split into two factions, clerical and anti-clerical. Lewis Y Pant, Mathew Thomas' son, was seen coming home one night, bloody but unbowed, followed by an excited mob of children, full of song and praise. Lewis had failed to see eye to eye with Teddy Y Nant about the respective virtues of the Rev. T. Cefnllech Roberts and the vicar of the parish. Teddy was an ardent churchgoer, and each of them was faithful to his belief unto death, and this caused a fight. Teddy went home alone and defeated, and full of woe; Lewis departed in glory, honour and rejoicing. The children escorted him to within sight of Y Pant, gave him three cheers and went away, leaving Lewis alone to explain the fracas to his mother. That evening the birch rod on the wall lost much of its foliage, but Lewis was not particularly worried about that. Even so, when he heard his father's two-tone supplication, during family prayers, become three-tone, for the first time ever, the third note floored him. He would have sworn on his knees to be an ardent tithe-supporter for ever, and that he would pay tithe on mint and anise and cummin, whatever these things might be — they figured in one of those Biblical verses that stuck in his memory; but, in his fright, he heard a sentence begging for divine protection for the heroes. The third note haunted Lewis for years like a nightmare.

There was a great to-do outside The Hand one evening, and the whole village got up to look. Harry Tŷ Draw and Isaac Y Llwyn could not agree on the respective worth of the Master of Pen y Bryn and Samuel Jones. Isaac was henpecked by his wife, and his wife was spellbound by Margaret Jones' eloquence. Harry was an old labourer from Pen y Bryn and he was defending the family honour. Each one took off his coat in the yard of the Hand, and men standing ready on each side held the coats. They braced themselves for the fray, shook hands, and started lashing out, and several people felt that a tithe war was a marvellous thing if this was how it began. Whereupon the priest came by, and he was brave enough, and unlucky enough, to join the crowd; for if Harry and Isaac were at loggerheads about their relationship to the Master of Pen y Bryn and Samuel Jones, they saw eye to eye about the priest. When he interfered, they turned on him. He was escorted home by the crowd with Harry and Isaac leading them. The end of the affair was that Harry reminded Isaac that he was a Congregationalist and Isaac reminded Harry that he was a Wesleyan. They swore eternal hatred of every other denomination until Tom, Y Rhyd Uchaf, came forward to remind them that the Calvinistic Methodists, too, were against the parson, and he was a Calvinistic Methodist. They then decided to form a triple union, so that they could take the country by storm in defence of their respective denominations. They swore eternal loyalty to one another in this noble campaign, and the three missionaries went home arm in arm, singing "I have a yellow pony," with the crowd following.

There was something pleasant about these waves — the first waves of the tempest — that were heard breaking on the shore. But some people sensed a more disturbing murmur in the breeze and they decided to try and remedy matters by encouraging the local people to hold a united prayer meeting on the first Monday evening of the month; failing that, everyone should spend the day on their knees. Great, strong, muscular men faltered before the heavenly throne that Monday evening, praying for succour and protection; or, if that were nor forthcoming, for strength to weather the storm without giving way or flinching. They looked for hymns that talked about succour and protection, and sang them all, and they ended up defiantly singing

"O! Arglwydd Dduw Rhagluniaeth, ac iachawdwriaeth dyn,
Tydi sy'n llywodraethu y byd a'r nef dy Hun."

("Oh Lord God, dispenser of providence and salvation, it is Thou who reignest over the world and over heaven.")

Everyone went home that night with renewed faith in the divine rule. And here and there, in the night silence, you could hear snatches of hymns wafting on the breeze from the valley, hill and woodland path, as if the Almighty were indicating from the great Beyond that he liked the singing.

Eventually the great wave came, and an auction was held at Y Bryniau, and Y Rhos Uchaf, and Y Tŷ Glas, and in turn the auction at Pen y Bryn. As each sale arrived, the people's hope and enthusiasm grew, until the climax was reached at the sale of Pen y Bryn.

Chapter VIII

A few boys and a man stood on the stone steps of the barn of the Crown on the morning of the auction. They waited for developments with bated breath and fiery eyes. It was a school day, true, and all of them, except the eldest and the youngest, were pupils, but they did not regard this as very important. Was not the very air electric with the spirit of defiance? Was not everyone thrilled by that spirit, and every other happening subordinate to it? And since the boys, too, had succumbed to the fever, they had played "truels" that day — schoolboy language for truant. Normally, no one would ever play "truels" but the bravest and toughest and most defiant, but when the country is in a fever the weak, too, are possessed by it, and very often they are the first to be possessed; and it raises them to the most supreme heights. In the crowd of boys there were weak ones and strong ones, each one just as fiery as the others, and as brave. This spirit transported them into a new world of seductive visions, a fine spacious world with far horizons, a world in which everything was alluring and dreamlike; its intoxicating freedom spelt death and contempt to authoritarian circles, and trampled down the laws of society without a glance — with that irresponsible, enjoyable abandon which comes at rare moments and makes life worth living.

There were some non-scholars among the lads — Jimmy, Mathew Thomas' son, and Hugh, Pant yr Afon. Jimmy was too young to start school, and Hugh was older than the schoolmaster. Jimmy had come to escort his brothers Peter, Mathew and Lewis a little way to school, and they met a number of their friends — and each friend was thrilled and inspired by the day's happenings.As they passed they saw Hugh, Pant yr Afon, in the yard of the Crown, and he strode over to them. He explained to them, in his own way, that he meant to spend the morning on the barn steps, and this prospect was so alluring that they all decided it was for them, too. From the barn steps you could see most of the roads and paths around, and desultory groups of three or four, of every age, tramping along them — some slow and hesitant, some in a mad hurry, and all bound for the Crown.

Soon a carriage was heard, and everyone within earshot quickened his pace at the sounds. The congregation on the barn steps nearly fell headlong to the ground — they were so eager to see the carriage. There were quite a few rather important-looking men inside, including a man in a white hat and gold-rimmed glasses. He had a gold chain across his chest and a number of gold rings on his fingers. He caused quite a lot of merriment. The carriage stopped at the Crown door, and its occupants quenched their thirst. But seeing the bystanders approaching and nudging each other significantly, and talking *sotto voce*, they judged it best to hurry on. Off they went towards Pen y Bryn, followed by a strangled cry from the mob, like the moan of a beast of prey cheated of its victim.

The children had long been asking each other — and Hugh — who this "tithe" was that everybody was talking about. They already had some glimmer, but these exciting occurrences called for a clear, definite view of the matter. Hugh did not know the tithe, and everyone was surprised, because Hugh knew everybody within miles of Llangeunant. Lewis thought he was the parson's brother. It was in the light of this revelation that he had a fight with Teddy, from Y Nant. When the carriage arrived, and everyone got excited, he decided it was the fellow with the rings and gold chain and the light-coloured hat. And since this kind of garb was unusual in Llangeunant, they decided that the tithe, however much people ran him down, was an extraordinary man. When the carriage had gone and the people had calmed down a bit, James the Crown's labourer, came up the steps to the barn. Everyone had to pass the Crown to get to Pen y Bryn, and everyone who was anyone stopped there for a drink, so they regarded James as the last word on all these topics. They made Lewis ask him whether the multicoloured gentleman in the carriage was, in fact, the tithe. James replied that the tithe was not a man but a place. But they could not understand why, if it was a place, you had to pay it, and why it was not mentioned in the geography book. In the middle of their arguments and discussions William Jones, Y Graig, came by. He was one of the eager crowd surrounding the Crown, and there was a rumour that the next auction would be at his home. Lewis asked him if he could please tell them where the tithe was. William Jones stopped short, and looked Lewis straight in the eye till he blushed to the roots of his hair. He went on looking at him till he shuffled his feet backwards and forwards and on top of each other, and finally tugged at his coat buttons and chewed his nails, his lips trembling. Lewis saw from William Jones' face that asking a sensible man about the tithe was something more awful than he had ever dreamed of.

"Well," said William Jones at last, slowly, "since you are so incredibly stupid, I must enlighten you, for the future good of Wales. The tithe is not a geographical location but a principle." Whereupon he took himself off. After this the children all remained quite still and mute for a long while, looking at each other, and thinking, and Hugh, who was with them, tried to follow suit. They realised that the world they were in was stranger than they imagined, and they threw furtive, uneasy glances towards the school, secretly suspecting that this, after all, was the safest place. They had never heard of principle, as far as they knew, it might well be something terrible, judging by William Jones' expression when he talked about it, and since it had to do with Wales of the Future. Hugh slunk away from them, and made for Pen y Bryn across the fields; Jimmy began to cry. Then they heard a heavy carriage, and the people — they were a crowd by now — stirred and moved excitedly around.

The lads craned their necks and saw the manes of two horses coming into view past the crossroads, followed by a brake full of policemen. Some of the bystanders shouted welcome, but a hail of mud fell on them which considerably dampened their enthusiasm. The brake of policemen went by, ignoring everybody, and the shuffling and weaving started up again, the boys clinging tightly to each other.

Soon a cloud of dust was seen rising over a hillock from the Coedargiodd Road, and a tramp, tramp, tramp sound approaching; someone shouted "Halt," and there was a great silence. Many faces grew pale, and many hearts palpitated, and yet no one wanted to run away. The boys squeezed up against the barn door as far as they could, and Lewis made sure the door was unlocked. Someone shouted over the hillock: "Quick march," and the steady, continuous, tramp, tramp, tramp started up again. About 200 miners from the lime quarries of Craig y Mwyn came into view, as orderly as an army of soldiers; each one had a spade, a crowbar, or pickaxe, or sledgehammer across his shoulder, like a gun. Every worker bearing a farm implement, whom they had picked up on their four-mile journey from Craig y Mwyn to the Crown, was with them. The look on their faces haunted everyone that saw them, for the rest of their lives. Their faces had that look — seen about once or twice in a lifetime — of the soul of a people awakening.

Two men carrying a banner led the miners, and a man with a long stick walked in front of them. When they reached the Crown, the man with the stick turned to them and yelled: ":Halt!" They all stopped in a twinkling, wiping their sweat with their caps. They had a bite to eat from their food tins and a drink from their bottles of tea. By now the crowd was raving mad, shouting and screaming and throwing hats and caps into the air. The boys jumped down from the top of the barn steps, oblivious of the steps and everything else, and started yelling and jumping and running. They lost each other in the fracas and everyone went his own way. Somebody ran towards Pen y Bryn and the crowd, like one man, ran after him — over hedges and fields and ditches full of water, just as if they were running on the open road; only the old folks and two or three children were left behind. After stopping to rest for a little, the leader of the miners' regiment shouted "Quick March" and the contingent was off again, in orderly fashion, as before; and they marched steadily and without pause to Pen y Bryn.

Jimmy and his brother Peter were among the children left behind. Jimmy cried and Peter looked miserable. They stood where they were for a bit, then Peter sent Jimmy home, and he himself went unwillingly to school; he was pretty late by now. They had both been searching the band of miners for their father, their little souls aflame with the heroism that electrified the atmosphere; but they had been unable to find him. A cold mist enveloped their lives and brought misery in its wake. As for Mathew and Lewis, they had not given their father a thought. They had been so preoccupied with doing something heroic themselves that they did not trouble about anyone else.

Going towards Pen y Bryn, a little behind the miners, you could hear a lot of shouting and laughing, and when you got within sight of it, you could see a gang of youths playing something which looked, from a distance, like a football, but when you got nearer it was plain that the ball was the light-coloured hat which had so charmingly adorned the carriage outside the Crown. The game did not last long, it is true, for a bullock rushed straight from the direction of the auctioneer's table, right through the yard gate and into the field. He made straight for the hat, as if to vent his spleen on the auctioneer. Neither team wanted the bullock on its side, so they left the game entirely, and made for the yard of Pen y Bryn in time for the big showdown.

The yard of Pen y Bryn was a square one, tidily enclosed with cowsheds and stables and a barn and pigsties; the house at the far end overlooked the valley beneath. The sale began quite peaceably. There were not many people there when the auctioneer arrived, and he managed to get under way without bother. The people gathered round the house, vast crowds of them. The police arrived and surrounded the auctioneer, and he felt safe. Finally the miners arrived. The crowd parted to let them through, which they did, in orderly fashion. Before anyone quite realised what was happening they encircled the policemen, though they kept a respectable distance from them. The Master of Pen y Bryn was standing about three yards from the door of one of the outhouses, with his back to it, looking thoughtfully towards the big oak tree that grew on a ridge overlooking the road which ran past the gate. The Rev. T. Cefnllech Roberts was at his side. Behind him stood a young man with an amiable expression, gazing in the same direction. Annie, Pen y Bryn's eldest daughter, was standing on the ridge, leaning on the oak; her face was pale and her gaze took in every corner of the yard. Her pallor made her eyes appear even more beautiful. It was daughter Annie that the Master of Pen y Bryn was looking at, and as he looked he was transported back to the time when her mother was just as beautiful, and her eyes just as bright; the world, then, was young and gay. And for a moment the Master of Pen y Bryn thought some of the beautiful, dynamic thoughts of life.

His wife was nowhere to be seen; she was sitting in the house crying. This, she supposed, was her most appropriate function on such an occasion. Lizzie, the youngest daughter, was comforting her. All the male servants were in the yard except Shôn Bach, and all the maids were in the house except Mary Eliza. Shôn had vanished, and none of the hoarse yells from the other manservants elicited a murmur from him. As for Mary Eliza, she stayed in the dairy longer, and more often, than was necessary, particularly on a day when there was so much to do; and the dairy was next door to the barn.

The first item brought forward for sale was a cow; despite the tension among the spectators, no one spoke, and no one lifted a finger to prevent her being sold. Every miner stood leaning on the implement he had brought. Hardly a sound was heard, except the water in the ditch in the yard, and the auctioneer's voice. His wisecracks descended on the crowd like a torrent; they fell on to it like water on to a rock, and the rock received it without wavering. As the silence grew more oppressive, the tension in the crowd increased. The cow was bought by an

Englishman who came with the auctioneer, then the little pony came up for sale. The little pony was one which Annie had ridden dozens of times, and everyone always linked them together in conversation. They all turned their gaze to Annie automatically, and the little pony turned its eyes towards her too, and neighed contentedly. Many hearts bled for Annie at this point, for she was very popular with everyone; they knew her tender heart and soft voice. The girl by the oak tree showed no reaction to all this, except that her pallor grew deeper than before; she did not move a muscle. The Englishman made a bid for the little pony; someone topped his bid; the Englishman made another bid, and the other bested him again. They were both strangers to the district. The neighbourhood was pretty well united in the agreement that no one was to help the auctioneer by bidding for anything. The Englishman soon got tired, and the auctioneer was about to knock it down to someone else when the amiable young man who stood at the outhouse door put in a higher bid, and the animal was knocked down to him before anyone had time to grasp the situation.

Everyone was amazed that the young man had made the purchase, because he was the son of Y Plas Isaf, and they had thought him very sympathetic to the anti-tithe faction. They were still stupefied while the pony was being taken away, and no one saw the young man again on the yard of Pen y Bryn that day. Everyone looked at Annie to see her reaction, but the only difference in her was that she blushed instead of staying pale.

After the little pony, a fine bullock was led out. Whereupon Hugh, Pant yr Afon, was seen pushing his way through the crowd to the front, and then he smiled amicably at the auctioneer as if they were old cronies. The auctioneer smiled back at Hugh in that nasty, inhuman way of his, and indicated that he should get some nuts to crack, since he was no longer fit for anything else. Before the last sentence had trickled past his lips, however, a lump of mud flew over the heads of the crowd, struck his hat and carried it for some yards into the midst of the youths already mentioned. Off they ran, yelling jubilantly, kicking the hat across the yard and through the gate and down the field. By now the tension in the crowd had become white hot. Many people were pale, but not through fear; you could feel that breathlessness you sometimes get in thundery weather when the storm is still far away in the mountains. The auctioneer was sarcastic, and hinted that Hugh was not the only one who would feel at home cracking nuts. One of the miners heckled him angrily; he was pushed back by the police, and the dam burst. The regiment of miners rushed forward with the crowd close behind them; they swept everything before them like withered leaves before a tempest.

The bullock ran berserk. He decided it would be less trouble to face the auctioneer's table than the crowd, so he put his horns beneath it, tossed it into the air, and belted through the gateway down the field to the players. Old Ellen Peters hardly had time to move her sweet stall before the bullock had raced past like a lightning flash. The police were quite helpless in the face of the great storm as it broke. Everyone fought and yelled, some standing and some lying down. William Jones, y Graig, was lying on the ground under the table, screaming hoarsely and demanding to know whether anyone had been killed apart from himself. No one listened to this philanthropic appeal.

The Master of Pen y Bryn stood with his hands to his ears, trying to convince every unbeliever, including those furthest away from him and the most vociferous, that the world was at an end and everybody was done for. Alternatively, he tried to rationalize the whole thing, in a persuasive, dovelike voice, to anyone who cared to listen to him — but no one cared to listen. In the midst of his efforts a gentle hand was placed on his shoulder: the hand of the girl who stood leaning on the oak tree a few minutes before. She led him to the house and he obeyed without demur.

When the youths had finished with the hat, they were ready to start on its owner, the Englishman, and one or two others of the same ilk, and they were escorted in a homeward direction, rather too speedily for comfort. The youths were aided by a bunch of drovers who had come to seek a day's work driving the animals that had been bought to their new homes. Since their hopes had not been realised, they felt they could not go home happily till they had driven something, at least, so they made the most of driving the auctioneer and his cronies. A crowd of policemen followed the mob, escorted by the miners. The policemen's action was not entirely voluntary, but after effective persuasion they accepted the situation and got moving.

A crowd of people stayed behind, not knowing exactly what to do. From a rational point of view, they entirely condemned the fracas, and emotionally they completely sympathized with it. One part of them wanted to go one way, and another part the other, so there was nothing for it but to compromise and stay put. And anyone who wished to could find sufficient justification for his action. Above the whole mêlée you could hear the hoarse voice of Y Bardd Crwst, the local bard, singing a revolutionary song. The poet would give a short spoken introduction, and each introductory piece contained some facts about the tithe auction; then, when the time came for him to exercise his poetic imagination, he would start rendering what was supposed to be a song. Things quietened down a lot when Y Bardd Crwst started doing his bit, but he hard barely finished when a well-known voice boomed from the other end of the yard, from the direction where the auctioneer had been attempting to conduct the sale, shouting "Fellow countrymen." The audience hurried back like one man to listen to this new voice.

It was the Rev. T. Cefnllech Roberts; he had set the table up again, and stood on it, and started to address the people's backs; but he soon saw their faces. "Dear fellow-countrymen," said the Rev. T. Cefnllech Roberts, and his words met with deafening applause. "This is a day never to be forgotten," he said, trembling all over with emotion, and again deafening applause followed. "The Philistines have been vanquished," he said amid increasing cheers, "and the chosen people have the boundaries of the promised land in sight." A great cry, louder than before, burst from the audience. It was plain to see that neither he nor his congregation bothered unduly about anachronisms, but what does that matter in a tithe auction speech? "The dawn is breaking," said the orator, practically hoarse and the applause was as appreciative as before; "it has broken," he said, and the people could no longer hold back when they heard this. "Shackles are being cast aside," said the orator when he got the chance, and from this point to the end the audience's yells of approbation were quite indescribable.

These were his final sentences: "The yoke of centuries of oppression is being broken; the mountains are bursting with song; the trees are clapping their hands, the flowers are dancing and the animals are leaping for joy, at the sight of Wales awakening." These were the greatest moments in the life of the Rev. T. Cefnllech Roberts.

When the minister had finished, the multitude rushed towards the house. Two or three of the strongest went in, and out they came with the Master of Pen y Bryn on their shoulders. Then they formed a procession, and down they went, singing "Land of my Fathers" towards Llangeunant, the leaders carrying the Master of Pen y Bryn on their shoulders. And these were the greatest moments in the life of the Master of Pen y Bryn, too. When they reached the Crown they took some tables and formed a stage, and another meeting was held; the strong ones had the Master of Pen y Bryn on their shoulders the whole time. Various people made speeches at the meeting, and judging by the orators and the enthusiasm of the audience, you would have supposed that the millennium was about to dawn the next day. For the children who played "truels" the millennium was simply a land without any school, and where there was a tithe war every day; for the mass of the crowd it meant the fun of running auctioneers and Englishmen out of the land.

No doubt the day would have ended on this note, and the Master of Pen y Bryn would have been borne home, as he had been borne to the spot, on the shoulders of the strong, followed by shouts of acclamation; the crowd would have been mad with joy, and the village band would have led the procession, had it not been for one incident. When the meeting was at the height of its fervour a carriage drew up, and a man whom everyone knew jumped out. If I named him, I would name someone known to the whole of Wales as one of the staunchest pillars of the movement. Another burst of applause broke out, the loudest of all, on his arrival; the poor fellow who was speaking at the time had to keep his observations to himself and join in the general welcome. The man climbed nimbly on to the stage and began to speak. His first sentence was: "Fellow countrymen, we are in the midst of a great battle," and this elicited the most deafening applause from the crowd. "A battle of principles," he said, and there was another shout. "But," he said, his eyes flaming, while their knees trembled beneath them, and they became like putty in his hands, "pelting auctioneers with stones and mud is not the way to win battles of principle." He got no applause for this; everyone stood thunderstruck, most with their mouths hanging open, and the Master of Pen y Bryn's throne-bearers lowered him, lightly and silently. The orator went on to lead his audience to the Far Distant Land, the land of the exalted and the magnificent vistas; they followed him as a flock of sheep follows a shepherd. The brilliant images he evoked made their eyes shine; his dark images made their eyes cloud over. One by one, he opened up the doors of their souls, and the breezes of the promised land were free to circulate in the rooms. He asked them to invite the Exalted Ones to come in, and to live in their company, and to listen to them, that they might share in their visions, partake of their strength, and dwell in their land for ever. Then, oppression and rapine would vanish and wither away, for the air where they dwelt would become too attenuated for them to breathe. The people's victory would be won with shining swords, not rusty, poisonous ones; and their swords would be the brilliant, shining flames of their own lives.

When the orator had finished his speech, they slunk off and went their own way, too ashamed to acknowledge their deeds of the day; they all felt pathetic and contemptible. But they all felt, too, that the doors of their souls were wide open, so that the Exalted Ones from the far distant land could come and visit. And the Master of Pen y Bryn was among those who walked home feeling like this. He could feel the gentle breezes in the open rooms of his soul, and he was sufficiently exalted, in the enthusiasm of the moment, to hear the voices of the divine beings, and to see them clearly enough to beckon to them, to ask them to come to him, if he wished. His future depended on that gesture. He was trembling on the threshold of a new life he had never seen nor imagined before; a world to whom John Williams and the Master of Pen y Bryn meant nothing, had he only known it. He was re-created, and he had found new companions. It was in this state of mind that he arrived at the house and faced his wife. He was regarded unequivocally in the neighbourhood as a hero, but was it really heroic, he asked himself in these moments, to part with an animal or two — if, indeed, he really had? Now, he imagined himself being put to the test: could he invite his wife to enter the open rooms of his soul to enjoy the breezes, and could he invite the exalted beings, whose pretentions were quite beyond him, to come along as well?

"John," said his wife — you could no longer see she had been crying — "marvellous, isn't it?"

"What's marvellous?" asked John Williams, his voice trembling.

"Marvellous how popular you are now," said his spouse.

"Yes," said John, closing the doors of his soul; the air in the rooms grew oppressive again. He breathed the same old air; the same old apathy was creeping over him again. And in that state of apathy, the Master of Pen y Bryn could appreciate his wife's banal conversation.

"Everyone was full of it," said Jane Williams, "even the servants. Did you see Shôn Bach with his red eyes? I'm sure the poor fellow had been crying; that's why he wouldn't show himself, even though everybody was shouting for him."

The Master of Pen y Bryn felt very proud that his heroism had brought tears to the eyes of his servants. Was not this a sign of their great admiration for him, and that in the people's view John Williams and the Master of Pen y Bryn were now one and the same?

True, little Shôn's eyes were red, but few tears had flowed from them that day, apart from those drawn by the wind as he looked through one of the cracks in the barn wall to see whether his master was safe in the yard, and through another crack to communicate with Mary Eliza, who spent most of that day near the dairy window, opposite one of the cracks in the barn wall. Shôn and Mary Eliza had been getting fond of each other for some days, and they felt that the day of the sale would be a wonderful opportunity to get together, one in the barn and the other in the dairy. Everyone was shaken to the core by the fever that swept through the land — all but Shôn and Mary Eliza.

At the end of the day, the Master of Pen y Bryn found it heartwarming to look into Shôn's eyes, thinking of the deep feelings that made him weep for his sake; and Shôn found it heartwarming, too, to look into the eyes of Mary Eliza and think of the emotions she betrayed that day at the dairy window.

Chapter IX

One fine morning after Evan Hughes, who led the singing in Bethania chapel, had been walking through the village, the stable door at the Bear, the cemetery wall and Bethania chapel door had one thing in common. There was a large poster stuck on each, and at the top, in big letters, the words "Bethania Chapel", and underneath the words "A grand concert will be held at the above place," and "grand concert" was bigger than anything else on the poster. No one passed through the village that morning without stopping at the Bear's stable door, or the cemetery wall, or the door of Bethania chapel, or at all three places. Some of them — members of the concert committee — would stop for just a moment, cast a very odd look at the paper, and rush off as if they had a train to catch. Others who stopped purely for information — prospective competitors, and the like — stayed longer. Others, too, stood there; people to whom such a poster was a novelty, the ones who had nothing to do but walk around looking for the chance to do good, like holding a horse's head, or some other small job, for twopence; and when no such opportunity arose, they propped up the walls, putting the world, and those in it who were out working, to rights. These people stood by the poster for a long time, and studied it carefully, wherever they saw it. It is unlikely that any of them could read a word, so they gathered round someone skilled in the art who had time on his hands, whenever such a person happened to be passing.

That particular morning, old Robert Morris, from the Turnpike, was the reader; he was out for a walk, leaning on his sticks. Robert Morris was not, it was true, a marvellous reader, but he was better than nothing. He adopted the method of half spelling out and half reading, and you had to stand there a long time if you had to rely on him for all the information on the poster. This suited the layabouts very well; time hung heavy on their hands, since they did not often find the opportunity to perform the good works which their qualifications fitted them for. When he had gathered an audience about him, Roberts Morris started reading. "B-e-t-h-a-n-i-a, Bethania," he said distinctly so that everyone could hear, "c-h-a-p-e-l, chapel, Bethania chapel," and so on. Robert Morris went on reading till he came to the words "Ch-air-man, chairman. John W-i-ll-iams, John Williams. Es-qui-re, esquire." "Dear me." said he to the company, "who would think that the old Pen y Bryn would get this far? I never thought, I must say, that there was so much to him," and off he went, hobbling along, leaning on his sticks, before anyone could reply.

There had been a lot of worry, sweat, argument and racking of brains behind the issue of this poster, and the wise men of Bethania held one meeting after another. The deacons and deaconesses, the choir leader and the minister were on the committee. Such a great undertaking was not to be entrusted to inexperienced youngsters. True, they had some kind of concert every year, but this was to be a much grander affair, in honour of its chairman. Everyone knew, before attending the first committee meeting, who was to fulfil this function, since the Rev. T. Cefnllech Roberts had had a tête-à-tète about him with each individual. Each one assured him that he would not mention the matter unless he heard something further about it; but everybody knew that everybody else knew. For the chairman's sake, therefore, prudence as well as knowledge was a vital commodity on the committee. No one except the minister and the choir leader knew any songs except tunes from the hymnal, and any knowledge of recitations outside the range of the hymn book was limited solely to the minister. When recitations were under discussion the minister had to stand in the middle of the floor, reading them one by one, as if he were reciting properly, then they weighed the pros and cons. The standard of adjudication was strange and varied, particularly when it came to the chief recitation. One recitation had the virtue of having "a lot of spirit", and the "spirit" was generated by the minister waving his arms about more vigorously when he read this one than when he read the others. The virtue of another recitation was that it was so obviously realistic; it was a piece about a mining disaster, and it naturally tended to make the ungodly souls in the audience think about their own end. This one got quite a lot of consideration; none of them knew very much about mining, but the Foty's manservant had been kicked by a horse the day before, and he was lying in bed dangerously ill. So everyone on the committee felt instinctively that something suitable for this sad occurrence should be chosen — the saddest occurrence in the neighbourhood for a long time. Before making a final decision, they resolved that certain standards must be followed, and that they should not accept any recitation which did not point out a moral; and pointing out a moral meant drawing attention to the Great Beyond and the Day of Judgement. Had not the Master of Pen y Bryn shown them, by his sacrifice, that material values were not the main thing; and was not the Foty's manservant, by all accounts, at death's door? These thoughts gnawed at the consciousness of everyone.

The minister spent hours reciting various pieces — patriotic, religious, witty, sombre, and terrible, but they eventually decided on "By the shores of mighty Jordan" as the chief recitation. Whereupon everyone nodded amiably and the minister scratched his head.

As far as the musical side was concerned, the choir leader and the minister got together to demonstrate the comparative merits of each tune. They stood in the middle of the floor, singing piece after piece, representing soloists, duettists, and finally a massed choir, and the committee sat in judgement. The final decision always wavered between patriotism and religion, and religion invariably won. After long consideration they decided that the chosen piece for the main choral competition would be "From the Hills of Jerusalem", after all, the Foty's manservant was terribly sick.

One member of the committee was in a bad mood throughout all the meetings — David Hughes the carpenter. Looking at people grimacing and listening to their awful singing was not his style, he said. But he was one of Bethania's wise men, and they had to have him on the committee. The minister begged him for his personal opinion, as he did with others like him, on every recitation and song, even though he knew in his heart that David Hughes' opinion was of little use on either. But he was one of Bethania's wise men. He had been sitting in one corner of the room, all hunched up, from the start of the meetings; saying nothing apart from a curt "yes" or "no" whenever someone asked him something; and he only got really roused once during the whole proceedings. Only one song ever touched his heart; and for all the world — however fond of the world he might be — he would never admit to anyone which song that was. Only one person knew of the circumstances: and she was — no, he would not mention her name, not even to himself. She was today, after all, the wife of the man who sat confidently before him. So that little romance would be buried with him — and with her, if she remembered anything about it and about that song. David Hughes began to reminisce, involuntarily, about the romance and the song, as he listened to the discussion about the singing; he pretended he was following it all in his own way.

"I have a song to suggest, very appropriate for those under eighteen," said Evan Hughes at some point in the discussion, after they had been making suggestions and singing for ages. David Hughes was hunched up morosely in his corner, listening without much enthusiasm, and Evan Hughes and the minister burst into song:

"Y, deryn pur â'r adain las,
Bydd imi'n was dibrydar,
O! brysur brysia at y ferch
Lle rhois i'm serch yn gynnar."

("Oh, gentle bird with blue wing, be thou my carefree messenger; make haste at once to the maid whom I loved when I was young.")

David Hughes stiffened in his corner; his eyes blazed feverishly; he listened for a moment in a trance, but when he came to he yelled out so harshly that he frightened everybody: "Fancy having a rotten song like that in a chapel concert!" The minister grew pale; Evan Hughes sulked for the rest of the meeting; and the two hastened, ungraciously, to suggest something else, and David Hughes sank back into his familiar shell. As he set off home that night, he wondered what *she* would think if her husband told her what happened at the meeting.

Finally, the programme was complete, and they set about choosing a chairman. The minister, as chairman of the committee, suggested they do this, and everyone looked at everyone else as if the idea of a chairman had never dawned on any of them. The minister went on to hint that one of their number had done them a great honour, and everyone looked still more bewildered and confused. Then the minister touched briefly upon the name of the Master of Pen y Bryn, and added one or two other likely names and everyone sank into deep contemplation. Soon, one of them proposed him tentatively, and after a brief silence the proposal was seconded, and he was elected unanimously. Then the minister asked whether anyone else had anything on his mind before they broke up the meeting. Mr. Price the shop, who had spent a lot of his time in England and who knew a great deal about these things, said he had something to put forward; they had not yet resolved that there was to be a concert that year.

Everyone's face fell — no, they hadn't passed a resolution on that, Mr. Price was quite right; and suppose someone were to propose, after all the hard labour and worry, that there should not be one this year? A great silence fell on them all, till you could hear a pin drop.

Mr. Price, seeing this, proposed that they have a concert, for the sake of formality, he said; he was supported, they passed a unanimous resolution, and everyone breathed freely again. They got up to leave. "It occurs to me," said the Master of Tan y Creigiau, who had been silent up to now, — and everyone sat down anxiously again, — "It occurs to me," he said again, "whether we should resolve that the items be limited to the whole world." "Open to the whole world, you mean," said John Owen the cobbler. "Yes, something like that," said the Master of Tan y Creigiau. "They have something like that on every programme I ever saw. My son sent one home from London recently, and there was something about 'limited to the world' or suchlike on it." "Open to the world," said the cobbler scathingly. "Yes, open to the world then," said the Master of Tan y Creigiau. And his suggestion was unanimously adopted.

At last, the concert itself took place; the doors were to be open at 6.30 and it was to start at 7.00. But the doors were open, in fact, all day, and the doorkeeper was there early in the afternoon. Half past six came, and a great multitude was seen through the length and breadth of the parish, but there was not a soul outside the chapel apart from the doorman and the minister. The uneasy sound of feet was heard, like the steady murmur of a river, from every direction, and the endless hum of voices, and horns sounding here and there. Soon, a carriage was heard approaching, and a big hurrah, and the crowd parted, and the Master of Pen y Bryn and his spouse were in the carriage, the pony trotting in front; and when they were near the centre of the village there was a drum drum drum, drum drum drum, from the direction of the Bear. The village band struck up, all together, and marched to meet them, and the horse reared up on his hind legs and danced to the sound of the band and the girls shrieked and everyone ran away, till two or three farm labourers came and leapt up on the horse to keep him under control. Then the band turned back, followed by the Pen y Bryn carriage and the crowd, who kept time instinctively to every beat of the drum with a frisky spring in each step, till they got to the chapel.

Jane Williams, after long practice in readiness for the occasion, had learnt how to smile graciously at the crowd, and her husband how to bow; and they performed their duty to a nicety. They got to the chapel at five to seven, and by seven the chapel was packed, and the concert began in the usual way; by singing what was termed "a hymn well known to all," i.e. "Beth sydd imi yn y byd?" ("What is there in this world for me?")

At the beginning the smallest children were called forward to compete in batches, to get them out of the way, before the chairman was called upon to deliver his address — and Jane Williams smiled at every child, and at everything and everybody. When the compère had listed, to his own way of thinking, the main qualities of the chairman, John Williams was called forward. The audience rose to its feet, went through the usual motions and sat down to listen; and the chairman began his speech. He called for sacrifice in the face of oppression and exploitation, and notified the audience that the day of the proletariat was dawning; and the audience got to its feet again to welcome its day, which was such a long time coming, in spite of all the advance publicity it had; and there the people were, waiting for it with the yearning of a mother for a long-lost child. The Master of Pen y Bryn called, once again, for sacrifice and courage and faith in the cause of the proletariat, and painted a rosy picture of the future; the audience became more and more enthusiastic, and he himself felt possessed by the fever, so bright was that picture. At the back of the chapel, in the cheapest rows, sat one who was absolutely mesmerized; one who, like many others in the neighbourhood, could not sacrifice more without starving. He did not understand the meaning of the word proletariat, much less know about the awakening of the proletariat; but he could see something before him which enchanted him, though he could not explain it, and he gazed at his old master open-mouthed, seeing him surrounded by a heavenly aura, like an angel, and slipping further away from his own little world the whole time; and this man was Mathew Thomas, Y Pant. He knew nothing of the proletariat or of heroism, only that his old master was someone extra special, living in a world quite strange to him; a world which attracted him greatly, though he had never understood it or ever been there. And he felt it was worth scraping a few pennies together to come to the concert and see the Master honoured.

After the chairman's address, the children's choir came forward under the leadership of Evan Hughes, and this was one of the most interesting items in the concert. All the parents who could come to the concert did so, to see their own children — more, even, than to see and hear the Master of Pen y Bryn. Evan Hughes had made meticulous preparations to ensure the success of the performance. The choir had been assembled in the schoolhouse before its cue, and it came on in orderly fashion, marching in time to the piano played by Evan Hughes himself. Each child had a paper hat with roses on.

The duet between the chief labourer of Pen y Bryn and the chief labourer of Ty'n y Foel was a bit of a disaster, though they had a good reputation as singers, and the muddle somewhat marred the evening's pleasure for the chairman and his wife, since the family honour was bound up with the success of the manservant. The song was "Betty Wyn", a popular ditty which was just becoming well-known in the locality; it was to begin with their singing in turns, then they were to sing the following words together:

"Os rhagluniaeth deg a'i myn,
Mi briodaf Beti Wyn,
Beti Wy-y-yn, Beti Wy-y-y-y-n,
O! Beti Wyn fy nghariad."

("If the gentle fates so wish it, I shall marry Betty Wyn; Betty Wyn my sweetheart.")

They proceeded without mishap up to the third line above. In the middle of it, the manservant of Ty'n y Foel broke off suddenly when he was on the verge of launching into the second Betty Wyn, and he stage-whispered to his partner, "You're going wrong." The other broke off quite as suddenly and whispered, "No, you are." "No, you," said the other. "No, you are," said his companion. A silent argument went on for a while, and the only signs the audience got were heads and mouths moving, like dumb cockerels trying to crow. They straightened themselves up eventually and started again. They were successful till they came to the second "W-y-y-y-n." "There you are again," said the manservant of Ty'n y Foel *sotto voce.* "No," said the manservant of Pen y Bryn, "it's you," and the mute argument started up again. Jane Williams blushed to see the family honour dimmed at the height of its glory; the chairman studied the programme with exaggerated interest; and the audience, out of respect to them all, looked embarrassed.

Suddenly, one of the singers launched into "Betty Wyn" on his own, oblivious of the audience, and anxious to show the other how it should be done; and he gave the most unearthly squeak. Poor Hugh, Pant yr Afon, could not contain himself, and he burst out laughing; the wave swept over the whole audience, so that the compère began to doubt his authority over them. When the laughter started the duettists stepped down, and the compère rose to announce the winner of the scythe handle competition. This was not, strictly speaking, the next item on the programme, but since the winner was one of the Foty's labourers, and the injured labourer was still dangerously ill, he thought the audience might sober up a bit if he referred to the Foty. Whereupon he received a note from someone in the audience, signed "One of the committee," suggesting that it would be most effective, after the scythe handle adjudication, to have the chief recitation competition; to drive the point home, as it were. So they had it. After which everything proceedded in a decent, orderly manner.

The labourer of Pen y Bryn regained his reputation, and the family honour survived unclouded, when he recited "The Big Pie of Llangollen." He made such a hit with the audience that the labourer from Ty'n y Foel was positively green in the face with jealousy. But as with everything else, not everyone took this recitation, even, in the same way. Miriam Davies, Tan y Creigiau, was astonished. "Fourteen sacks of flour, just to make the crust, Harry love!" she said to her husband. "Is it true, do you think?" "True? Of course it is," said her husband, "or the fellow wouldn't say so in a place like this," and he proceeded to listen. The chief labourer scored such a mighty success this time that he restored Jane Williams' new-born grandeur to its full glory.

This was not the only concert in the village that night — any more than at any other time when an official concert was held. There was an open-air concert, too, held by those who found it more amusing to have their own entertainment outside than to be indoors under the authority of others; besides, it was cheaper. As things went with a swing indoors, voices were heard outside proclaiming hoarsely that the Master of Pen y Bryn was the man for them, no matter what anyone said: and they expressed their feelings in this way:

"Gŵr Pen y Bryn i ni, Gŵr Pen y Bryn i ni,
Waeth beth a ddwedo undyn, Gŵr Pen y Bryn i ni."

("The Master of Pen y Bryn for us (twice); no matter what anyone says, the Master of Pen y Bryn for us.")

The tenor drew out the word "undyn" (anyone) in the most melting and dulcet tones. They alternated this song with another, just as effective. There were about 16 verses to this song, as far as one could calculate, but they can be judged by quoting just two verses, since they all follow the same line of reasoning. The first verse was:

"Bûm yn canlyn injan ddyrnu hyd y wlad, — hyd y wlad,
Bûm yn canlyn injan ddyrnu hyd y wlad, — hyd y wlad,
Bûm yn canlyn injan ddyrnu, bûm yn canlyn injan ddyrnu,
Bûm yn canlyn injan ddyrnu, hyd y wlad."

("I followed a threshing machine throughout the land, throughout the land (twice); I followed a threshing machine, (three times), throughout the land.")

And the second verse:

"Do, bûm hefo injan ddyrnu hyd y wlad, — hyd y wlad,
Do, bûm hefo injan ddyrnu hyd y wlad, — hyd y wlad,
Do, bûm hefo injan ddyrnu, do, bûm hefo injan ddyrnu,
Do, bûm hefo injan ddyrnu hyd y wlad."

("Yes, I was with a threshing machine," etc.)

It was the base part that took up the second "hyd y wlad" ("throughout the land") in these verses, and it would chime in vigorously and effectively each time.

The concert went on for a long time, in full swing, a mixture of singing and throwing matches with coloured flames into the air. Then the main item of the indoor concert was announced — a performance of "The Prodigal Son"; something new to the area. Everyone who was outside rushed to the chapel door. The performance was virtually an unqualified success. True, the elder son was younger than the Prodigal Son, and the father was younger than both, but it was a play, and it had a moral. The bit where the Prodigal Son was pondering on what to do with his share of the estate was most gripping. He decided that he would travel first class in the train, that he would go to the most important theatres and the best public houses. Strangely enough, although they were situated in the Orient, the theatres and public houses all had well-known English names. The Prodigal Son went to a far distant land wearing a red cap; the way there was up one aisle of the chapel, through the audience, and everybody made way for him; not a soul tried to persuade him that he was going astray. When he reached the door, i.e. the far distant land, he turned his coat inside out, and came back down the other side of the chapel, wearing a round, hard hat instead of the red cap, without much of a brim; a hat which is usually termed a bowler. Very strange, the dress these Orientals go in for! There was only one mistake — a tiny one — throughout the performance. The Prodigal Son came back from the far distant land too soon, and his father was not ready for him, and was still in the middle of his soliloquy of longing for him; and the Prodigal Son had to stand in the middle of the chapel till his father had finished. And there was the father, looking over the lad's head into the great beyond, shading his eyes from the sun with his hand, pretending not to see him anywhere. It was more important for the father to finish his monologue than to welcome his son back, and he did not remember the words very well. But all in all it was a most successful performance, and everyone was well pleased, and it was generally felt that the concert in honour of the Master of Pen y Bryn was worthy of the occasion.

When the programme was over, the chairman and his spouse

got three rounds of applause from the audience inside and the audience outside, though the outsiders had not experienced any of the concert apart from the opportunity of welcoming the Prodigal Son to their ranks for a brief while at the chapel door. They sang "Land of my Fathers" and the chairman and his wife set off for home, followed by the whole audience. They followed them right up to their door, and left them there amid great rejoicing.

The Master of Pen y Bryn was satisfied with his evening, and his wife more satisfied still; the plan had worked out admirably. The local people, too, were satisfied. Before the tithe war, when they thought of John Williams, they used to think of a querulous, superficial, unreliable and ungrateful man; when they thought of the Master of Pen y Bryn, they thought of a man of old and dignified lineage, one of the oldest and most dignified in the land. No one announced that, from now on, there was to be a change; instinct is so powerful that everyone automatically stopped mentioning John Williams and the Master of Pen y Bryn, — he was now Mr. Williams, Pen y Bryn, to everybody. He was now completely integrated with his own legacy of the past, in the eyes of the neighbourhood. And it was this which pleased the Master of Pen y Bryn.

As they went home that night, Mathew Thomas, Y Pant, stood cap in hand at the roadside, his back to the cemetery wall, watching the whole scene with bewilderment. He went home pondering on the indescribable greatness of being a hero. He went home to bed, so that he would be prepared to go out to work next day; to toil away calmly and without complaining, to keep a wife and five children from need, for a few shillings a week, quite alienated from the festive atmosphere of that evening. He would suffer the lack of an occasional meal, and a suit of clothes, for their sake; and he would never, never, see anything strange in this.

Chapter X

There are some pleasant hours of summer when the sea seems still, completely still, without as much as a wave in motion, or the lightest swell on its surface. A half-dreamy visitor on its shores might suppose that its regular, incessant movement had ceased for ever and that the sea, at last, was being left in peace, instead of being perpetually pulled upwards. He might suppose, too, that the moon, losing hope of attracting the sea to her sphere, had let it rest according to its wish. And the visitor, who knows of the tempests and tragedies of the sea, finds this a comfort: seeing the sea, of all things, in a quiet mood. But as he goes on gazing, it is not long before he sees a little wave rising in the distance, a wave which he did not expect in the enchantment of peace; but a wave which completely destroys the equilibrium of the sea, when it does come. And again the sea starts its uneasy, constant, ceaseless motion, obeying the çall from above. And this story is the story of a wave breaking, on a lovely summer's day.

The Master of Pen y Bryn stood in the yard, his hands in his pockets, on a fine spring day, four or five days after the concert at Bethania. He hummed contentedly to himself, and felt that he and the whole world understood each other perfectly. He had just come back from the fields, having put the labourers to work; he had noticed for some time that their obedience, and respect for him, were growing all the while. He was almost a god to his wife and family; and the young men and girls bowed and curtseyed to him more deeply than ever. He was a hero in the eyes of the world, and he had bought his birthright cheaply. In fact, the bargain was such a good one that he congratulated himself on it, often and with enthusiasm. He was half smiling on this particular morning, remembering that peculiar night when he threatened to leave his farm and, in a weak moment, went and asked David Hughes the carpenter and Mathew Thomas, Y Pant, for advice on the matter. He smiled more broadly still, thinking how he had managed to avoid David Hughes the carpenter so successfully afterwards, even though the other got weary of seeking him out. He knew it was quite something to scorn the advice of David Hughes, who had such a reputation as an adviser. He stopped humming and started whistling, inspired by the feeling that this, too, had been most heroic of him; and it was pretty unusual for the Master of Pen y Bryn to hum or whistle.

As he was about to turn in, he could see someone coming into view past the hedge at the bottom of one of the fields, and walking slowly and calmly up the path to the house, as if he had all the time in the world; so much, indeed, that he did not know what to do with a good half of it. The Master of Pen y Bryn knew, from his step, that it was the postman, and he went to lean on the yard gate to wait for him. He had several chats with him recently by the yard gate, because he had received more letters recently than at any time in his life. They came from far and near, from strangers and acquainances, to congratulate him on his heroism. He liked to open them at the gate and read the purple passages to the postman. And this particular morning, he waited for him as eagerly as on the previous mornings, and the other approached, step by step, till he reached the gate. He gave the eager recipient a number of letters; he opened them one by one and saw, as he did so, that they too were letters of congratulation. He read the juciest bits aloud and the postman reciprocated by telling him the local gossip — what this one and that one thought of him. He, when he got the chance, asked what David Hughes the carpenter thought, for he knew that he influenced local opinion in this as in everything else. The postman had not heard a word from David Hughes, so he just concocted an opinion, and it was a favourable one. The Master of Pen y Bryn rewarded him by telling him to go to the house for a bit of bread and cheese and some mead to help him on his way; he had done this every morning for quite a while. As the postman walked off he came across another letter; he was so excited that he called on him to wait a little. He started reading the letter to himself first; he grew pale, his hand shook, and he opened and shut his eyes alternately, as if a mist were rising between him and the letter. The postman saw that this was not, to say the least, a letter of congratulation, and off he went to get his bread and cheese and mead. He went his way after finishing his snack, pretending not to see the Master of Pen y Bryn, who was still standing just as he had left him. The postman went on to the fields to look for the chief labourer. He had been getting letters recently, too, but it was obvious that they were not getting to him directly, because this particular one had a note on the corner, in a hand which looked as if it were more at home with a broom or a floor-rag than a pen: "Put it to the man himself."

The Master of Pen y Bryn went on standing where he was, just where the postman had left him, trying to understand that letter — and in vain. The letters danced in front of him; the lines ran into each other; the mist between him and them deepened. A cold shiver ran over him and he trembled from head to foot, his teeth chattering, like a small, naked child out in the dead of winter. He clutched the gatepost to save himself from falling. The mist grew so black around him that it became utter darkness, and he felt himself sinking, sinking into a deep chasm; a black, silent chasm without a ray of light or a human voice. He kept sinking all the time, groping for something to clutch at. He found something, but it sank down with him. In the end his fall grew slower and eventually ceased.

The darkness was cloven; the light came again; and he found himself leaning on the gate, clutching it so passionately that the flesh on his hands became blue-black. He saw his letter on the ground at his feet. He could not pick it up for a while, but after mustering up all his strength he succeeded, and read it again — character by character, word by word. The letters danced again, and the lines ran into each other, try as he might; and fearing that the darkness and that awful sinking feeling might recur, he put the letter in his pocket and left the spot. He crossed the yard in as sprightly a way as he could, and off he went to the little grove near the house — an old grove which was inextricably linked with his life and traditions. In the heart of the grove was an old, fallen tree trunk; he sat down lifelessly and read the letter again. He read it slowly, character by character, then read it again from the beginning; he did this scores of times before he managed to get right through it once. At last he managed to finish it and held it a long time in his hand. He looked at it, then read it through again, glaring at each word, as if there should be some covert meaning in some word which would transform the meaning of the whole letter. After reading it many times he looked into the wood without seeing it at all, his face white as chalk and his hand trembling. Figures danced before his eyes; some mocked him, some sympathized, and they all sped along so fast that he could not tell which was which. During these moments he called his father's name, and his mother's; his age did not stop him. In times of trouble, a man becomes a child again.

He sat on the tree for an hour, two hours, oblivious of time and of everything except the letter and the dancing figures. The document had made such an impression on him that he could see it in front of him in big characters, and he read it word for word in space; the actual letter was still folded in his hand. There he stayed, till the sound of the dinner bell stirred him. When he heard it he got up, put the letter in his pocket separately from the other letters, tried to appear as normal as possible, and went in. He ate his dinner with as good a grace as possible, but he kept putting his hand in his pocket all the time, fingering the letter; then he would draw his hand back as if it were too hot to handle. After dinner he went back to the grove to sit on the old tree trunk, and think, and read the phantom letter in space.

As we have seen, David Hughes, some time previously, had been to Y Ddôl to see his brother Richard, to ask him if he wanted a bigger farm, so that he could think out his advice to the Master of Pen y Bryn about retiring from farming. And his brother had answered with a question.

"Sir John's land, or the bishop's?"

And David Hughes' reply, as we know, was:

"The Bishop's."

There was a lot of uncertainty in the neighbourhood about the ownership of much of the land. Sir John was the bishop's brother, and most of it was his; the bishop had much less. But Sir John was a wild and prodigal brother who had several times mortgaged away parts of the estate, and the bishop had managed the lot, more than once, while Sir John was far away from his native land, no one knew where. The rent was paid to the bishop's overseer and the land was let through him; rumours often circulated that the estate had all fallen to the bishop's ownership, because Sir John was dead, murdered, bankrupt or something of the sort. But Sir John would appear again in his homeland from time to time, and uncertainty about his rights to the land flared up again. People knew that parts of the estate had already been transferred to the bishop, but nobody knew which parts they were, except those with a special interest. At one time, Sir John was the owner of Pen y Bryn, and even though there had been frequent rumours that he had made the place over to the bishop, local opinion associated it with Sir John, and it was of him that people thought instinctively when the landlord was mentioned. He was the more popular of the two landlords because he was less likely to be bothered, or to bother anyone else about his convictions — for the simple reason that he had none.

The Master of Pen y Bryn was one of those people who never think about the landlord except on rent day. In the excitement of that period, the idea of his landlord had not crossed his mind; even when he did think of him, his ideas were a bit vague. The only thing which preoccupied him was his insane desire to do something which would put him in the good books of his fellows — to know that they respected him for himself, not his status. He had become obsessed to fever pitch with this urge; he would have done anything for it. And yet: the letter he received that morning was a burden too great to bear. It said that, within an appointed time, the farm of Pen y Bryn would go to someone else, and that pretty soon; it had, in fact, been promised to someone else, and it was hoped that he would be more loyal to his landlord that the present tenant.

He sat on the old tree trunk for a long time that afternoon; then he suddenly got up and walked around like a somnambulist till teatime; and when they called him he could not understand why the interval between dinner and tea was so incredibly short.

Jane Williams had noticed her husband's mood for some time. At first she thought he was suffering from one of his usual fits of depression, but then she saw that he had a piece of paper in his hand every time she saw him, crumpled out of all recognition. Evening came and they were left alone; everybody else had gone his own way. They sat for a long time, one gazing into the fire and the other looking at her over his glasses, forming a lump in her cheek with her tongue. Neither said a word. You could only hear the fire crackling and the clock ticking, and a spider making a similar ticking noise as he spun his web. Then Jane Williams put her hand in her husband's and drew out the slip of paper; he opened his hand to her willingly enough. She read it, after which she was pale, too. But some creatures, however ordinary, have a very strong instinct for self-preservation, and Jane Williams was one of them. She rose and sat by her husband's side, put her arm round his neck, and propounded a plan to him. It was a simple enough plan; the sort of plan people like herself would naturally think of, and also the most likely to succeed — if it could be kept a secret.

The next morning, the Master of Pen y Bryn left by the first train for the seaside, for a little rest after the troubled time he had just gone through, and to get ready for the busy period. Many had gone before him days ago, among them David Hughes the carpenter and his brother, Richard Hughes, Y

Ddôl. The bishop's palace and office were at the seaside, quite near the town they were all bound for.

In a few days the Master of Pen y Bryn came back from the seaside in a much better mood. Every limb radiated health and strength, and everyone congratulated him because the sea had done him so much good. Indeed, he had received a lot of benefit, but not so much from the sea, as everybody thought. They regarded the sea as harbouring in its bosom all the secrets of health. For they were folk who lived far away from the sea; many of them had never seen it.

The first morning after the Master of Pen a Bryn got to the seaside, the first thing he did was look for the bishop's office, and try to get round the overseer, but the fellow was adamant. Nothing would move him. The new tenant was satisfied with the deal, and was waiting for final confirmation. The Master of Pen y Bryn had to leave; he was disappointed and his prospects looked bleak. But another door was open to him; that of the palace itself, and he went there without delay. He was summoned to the bishop's presence, and the great man sat there in all his majesty, waiting for him. He told him humbly who he was and what he wanted. The bishop looked through a list of names on his table, and when he saw the Master of Pen y Bryn amongst them he wrinkled his forehead and frowned self-righteously at him. The other trembled in his presence like a captured bird. With all the force of ardent cowardice, he stressed how faithful his family had been, for generations, to the bishop's family; and in view of this he pleaded to be allowed to stay on at Pen y Bryn, but to no purpose. Then he pushed his spouse's plan to its limit — or beyond it. He fell on his knees and dissociated himself entirely from the crazy act which had brought him to this pass: not paying the tithe. He pleaded his lack of common sense and his blindness, which had stopped him seeing things in perspective. He begged again for forgiveness, just this once, and swore never again to transgress the will of the great man in any way. The bishop let him stay in that condition for quite a time; just as some people say that the Almighty does not answer a prayer, because He really enjoys seeing the penitent pleading before Him. Then he ordered him to rise, and extracted from him another vow that he would not offend against the law again; then he sent him to his overseer with a note to the effect that John Williams was to remain tenant of Pen y Bryn.

On his way from the bishop's office, John Williams met many strangers and acquaintances, taking a walk from the seaside town where he himself was staying. *He* was just coming back from his walk, he said. When he reached the outskirts of the town he met David Hughes, the carpenter, and his brother; they were going for a walk too. David Hughes said he was sorry he had not known earlier that the Master of Pen y Bryn was going that way for a walk; he could have had their company. But since he was not keen on turning back with them at that hour, there was nothing for it but for them to turn back with *him*, so as not to break up the party. But before nightfall, David Hughes and his brother had been for a walk that same way — without the Master of Pen y Bryn. They all went back home in a few days; the Master of Pen y Bryn was doubly joyful because he was a popular man locally for his heroism, and because he could feel certain of being allowed to stay at Pen y Bryn despite all efforts to shift him. He slept peacefully on his first night at home.

Chapter XI

It was two o'clock in the morning; the translucent quality of the moonlight in early May made the countryside look magical and spectral. There was still a layer of winter snow on Rhewyn's highest peaks. Over the whole area, up Peilliad and Gwynfar Valleys, and over the plains and distant hills right to the farthest horizons, the hedges round the geometric fields looked like a gigantic net thrown over the landscape; the land found its servitude so attractive that it slept peacefully and contentedly under its spell. You could see, on hill and meadow, the white frontages of cottages and farmhouses gleaming in the moonlight; everything was peaceful, inside and out. There were clumps of blackness here and there in the fields — the farm cattle lying quietly, with many hours to pass before man called them. You could hear them chewing the cud occasionally from the nearest fields; the only sound apart from Ceunant river breaking the silence of the night. Occasionally one of the animals would rise, and wander aimlessly backwards and forwards as if it were sleepwalking; then it would lie down again to chew the cud or go to sleep. Sometimes a gentle breeze would come wafting from some grove, bearing a puff of early summer perfume; then the air would be calm and sleepy again. As the moon began to wane the shadows of the trees and the hedges and the cows lengthened, as if some magic were making them grow, and they intermingled one by one; and as the moon vanished all the shades became one great, oppressive shade over the whole countryside. It bore an audible wave of melancholy with it.

As the last rim of the moon faded from view, a new sound broke the silence; such a little sound that none but the initiated would have noticed it. It was a muffled barking coming from the nearby hills; it ceased when the faintest breeze rustled. Soon, light appeared in bedroom windows, in this farm and that; then the light passed down to the kitchen, and a man came out of practically every farmhouse. However soft that barking, it was not too soft to wake any farmer, even the heaviest of sleepers. It is very seldom that a farmer fails to do this.

The next morning, the farmers sought each other out; then they went in twos and threes towards the village. When they arrived they got together and went into conference. Each one had his dog at his heels. Every now and then they would turn and look at their dogs, and every dog would raise his eyes and look his master straight in the eye, as innocent as a dove. Then the discussion resumed, with everybody talking at once. Three of Y Fron's lambs had been killed, and the Hafod sheep had been disturbed, so that they strayed all over the place; a few sheep who were late in lambing were in danger of their lives. The men had not been there a moment before the whole village was out, and the story of the sheep-killer dogs spread like wildfire. It grew as if by magic, like the night shadows beneath the moon. Every kind of suggestion was made, possible and impossible, but the one which met with the most scathing reception was someone's idea that everyone should tie his dog up for a night or two. No farmer who had any affection for his dog could think of tying him up, any more than he could let a bosom friend go to prison without a charge being preferred against him. In the end they decided that they should keep watch, in twos, for a few nights, and follow the dogs home if they were caught.

The following night, the Master of Y Fron and the Master of Yr Hafod had volunteered to keep watch. They started off before the moon began to wane, and hid on the mountain under a tree, in the middle of Y Fron's sheep and the Hafod's sheep. The two flocks were on the same side of the mountain. They stayed there a long time, till daybreak, and still nothing had come near to disturb the sheep, who grazed peacefully around them. A little before dawn, they thought they heard a muffled barking in the distance, but although they listened carefully they did not hear it again, and in the end they decided it was imagination. At dawn they went back home. Early that morning the local people heard the news that the Tŷ Glas sheep had been disturbed in the night, one or two sheep brought to death's door, and a number of lambs killed. There was another conference; each man had his dog at his heels, looking perfectly innocent. The mystery deepened every minute. Were the dogs from another locality perhaps? Such things had happened. They decided on two teams of watchers that night.

The Master of Y Fron and the Master of Yr Hafod said they would keep watch again, and the Master of Y Bryniau said he would keep watch with the Master of Y Tŷ Glas on the other side of the mountain. They kept careful watch, but not a rustle or murmur was heard, only the sheep, grazing and chewing away happily, and they went home contented. No more killings were heard of that morning, but later in the day the Master of Y Warchae came to the village, obviously alarmed. Two lambs and a sheep in his fields, he said, had been slaughtered during the night.

The mystery continued to deepen. The number on guard duty increased every night, and in the end each farmer guarded his own flock, since no one knew where the killings would break out next. The sheep on two farms had been left alone — Y Foty and Pen y Bryn. Gradually, people got a bit suspicious of Shep, Y Foty, and Rover, Pen y Bryn. The only foundation for this suspicion was that no sheep had been killed on either of these two farms, and a dog will not attack his own flock. But in spite of endless investigations, no one could find the slightest reason for suspecting Shep or Rover. As the guard duty became general the killings stopped, but the moment any flock was left for a night without a guard, sure enough, you would find dead lambs or sheep there the next morning. One night, when the Master of Y Fron and the Master of Yr Hafod had been on guard so long that they dozed off, they heard the sound of running, and the sheep raced wildly past them. They leapt up like bloodhounds over the sheltering ridge, but too late: they saw two dark shadows vanishing between them and the sky, streaking past a clump of heather. When they reached the spot, there was no sound anywhere — only the sheep, which had clustered together in the shelter of a rock, looking scared, and breathing heavily and quickly.

The mystery was deepening, deepening all the time. In the end, they decided to watch the dogs, and on those nights there were no killings. The Master of Y Foty and the Master of Pen y Bryn testified, like the others, that neither of their own dogs — Shep or Rover — had tried to leave the yard at all, though they did not know they were being watched. After a week or two without killing the guard duty slackened off, but one morning the neighbourhood was alarmed by the news that a number of lambs from Pen y Bryn had been killed during the night. This exonerated Rover from the slightest suspicion, and anyway he was none too well these days, and he had been kept home at nights for some time. More mysterious than ever! The Master of Y Fron and the Master of Yr Hafod testified that they had seen *two* dogs; the only two under suspicion were Shep and Rover, and now Rover was innocent. There was a country wide watch for nights after that, but no one heard or saw anything, not since that night when the Master of Y Fron and the Mater of Yr Hafod saw the two shadows vanishing past a clump of heather. There was no more killing.

The guard slackened off again. But in a couple of evenings, in the dead of night, the silence was shattered by shouting and barking and a horrible tearing sound. Every farmer and labourer within earshot leapt out of bed and went to investigate. The sounds came from the fields of Pen y Bryn, at the foot of the mountain. They stopped for a moment, then started up again, more horrible than ever, and as every new cry broke upon the air everybody quickened pace. The sound had died away completely before anyone got to the spot, and they had to search the place for some time. Pen y Bryn's sheep were in the lowest corner of the field, packed close together; they seemed terribly frightened. The crowd raced to the upper corner of the field. The sight which confronted them, in the first light of dawn, was one they would never forget. A lamb lay dead, bleeding from the throat. There was a black shape lying a short distance from it; it was neither sheep nor lamb. It was the corpse of Shep, Y Foty. Rover, from Pen y Bryn, was sitting over him, too weak to stand. He was covered with wounds and his jaws were stuffed with Shep's hair. Shep's jaws, too, were stuffed with the lamb's fleece and Rover's hair. Everyone stood silently, looking down at the carnage, and slowly the truth dawned on them. The Foty's dog was the culprit; and Rover had been watching him. This was why the Pen y Bryn flock had been left in peace until Rover fell ill. And who would have thought it of Shep Y Foty?

Seeing his faithful old dog, his companion on the mountains throughout the years, in such a state, and seeing that — worst of all — he had died in disgrace, the Master of Y Foty burst into tears. He sighed deeply and sorrowfully; his tears flowed like a river. And even though every farmer present had suffered loss through Shep, there was not a soul who could fail to sympathize with him with all his heart; for they all knew what the friendship and fidelity of a dog meant. They all stood there looking at him, saying nothing; his tears went on flowing, his heart almost torn asunder. And the dawn broke on a sad little band that morning.

The Master of Y Foty was, in fact, the first to move. He went over to Shep, lifted him up on his shoulder and went away, without a word to anyone. The crowd stayed where they were, silent and still, watching him move away between them and the dawn; and a thrill transfixed them when he stopped for a minute on the brow of the hill, to rest and re-arrange his burden. The hill was dark beneath him, and he, with his dog on his back, was a black cipher between them and the rosy dawn; a figure magnified to unusual proportions by the strange light. They almost felt that one of their old gods of ancient time was standing there in judgement over the land. And such was the awe that fell upon them that they stood there for a long time to gaze at him, without moving a muscle. When he had disappeared over the hill, each man sighed and turned to speak to his neighbour.

They went to Rover and caressed him, and he relaxed when he felt their caresses; he began to wag his tail and gain strength. Rover was praised to the skies, and anyone in the crowd who had a dog even remotely related to him swelled with pride and explained the relationship. The Master of Pen y Bryn carried the lamb home, and the other farmers helped Rover on when he slowed down and showed signs of fatigue. But there was something else, mingled with the admiration for Rover, which was to the neighbourhood's credit; a deep and sincere sympathy for the Master of Y Foty, for they all understood what a man must feel when his dog has let him down, and it becomes common knowledge.

But — the killing did not cease. After Shep's death no one bothered to keep watch any more; everyone thought the problem had been solved at last. There was peace for a few days, and everybody felt relieved. But one morning they heard that some lambs from Y Bryniau had been killed during the night, and the neighbourhood was in a bigger quandary then ever. The two dogs which the Master of Y Foty and the Master of Yr Hafod had seen were both killers, after all. Who was the other dog, and where was he when Rover killed Shep? If he was with Shep, why did he run away instead of helping him? But, as the saying goes, it is the guilty that flees when no one persecutes him, and one honest dog is stronger than two guilty ones. The discussions and the laborious guard duties started up again. This time, they started with every farmer looking after his own sheep; but when killings did take place they were far less generalized. The Bryniau sheep, and the ones on their side of the mountain, were the ones attacked. People started watching in pairs again, and each pair was allocated a particular night; but although there was always a killing somewhere they did not catch anything. In the end, they decided to chain the dogs. One night, it was the turn of the Master of Pen y Bryn and the carpenter, David Hughes, to keep watch. The carpenter, too, had his sheep. Late that night — too late to find anybody else — David Hughes sent word to say he was not sure if he could come; the Master of Pen y Bryn should set out first, and he would follow him later if he could, since he had a coffin to finish.

At about one o'clock in the morning the Master of Pen y Bryn went to see if Rover was all right; he found him sleeping beside his chain. At first he thought of taking him along, but then he left him there and set out. He made his way, step by step, up the narrow path with high hedges on each side that led to the mountain. It was a very fine night; a quiet like the quiet of the grave reigned over the earth. A dread seized him as he walked, particularly when a rabbit scuttled quite unexpectedly across the path; he could not help but think of David Hughes and the coffin he was making. When he had gone a little way he heard a chain rattling near the ghostly old oak, and a cold shiver passed through him; but on investigating he found that it was the mill's donkey grazing along the hedge, dragging his chain round his neck after him. Gradually, he got to thinking of his own life, and the glory that surrounded him; but it did not seem as romantic now as it did on the night of the concert. Nature around him at that moment was so single-minded, somehow, that the splendour of the night of the concert seemed empty and meaningless. He remembered the morning when he pleaded with the bishop, and although he smiled to think of his victory over his hidden enemy, he could not rejoice greatly in his triumph. He stood leaning on Ceunant Bridge for a moment, deep in thought, asking himself: had John Williams and the Master of Pen y Bryn actually become one and the same person? Was there not something strangely integrated in everything around him? And so he stood on Ceunant Bridge, forgetting what he had come for, till he was aroused by something falling into the water, as if some creature were jumping into it. He went on.

As he was approaching the foot of the mountain, he was disturbed by the sound of something running in panic; he could see the sheep rushing over a ridge and stopping to look back, standing between him and the grey-black sky. He scrambled over the mountain ridge on his hands and knees, thus dragging himself along the ground as quietly as he could. He stopped a moment to listen, and he heard a ravenous, sucking sound not so far away. He dragged himself forward again and the sucking sound grew louder as he approached; he knew at once that there was only a little clump of heather between it and himself. "At last," he said, "we've caught the killer. But how can I get hold of him before he gets away? And how to recognise him?" And the cruel, gluttonous, devouring sound went on, the other side of the heather.

When he thought he was within close enough range, he leapt to his feet, and was on the other side in a flash. He found a dead lamb, with a dog at its throat, sucking for all he was worth. The dog, too, started up when he saw the man, and growled viciously and threateningly. But when the Master of Pen y Bryn saw the dog on his feet and recognised him, he felt too limp to lay hands on him, and he sank down on the patch of heather, his head in his hands. No, he could not pluck up the courage to do anything to him. Somehow — he could not explain it — he felt a certain sympathy for the dog; the creature had been caught doing something so different from anyone's conceivable opinion of him. He raised his head. The dog was standing his ground and growling; he had never met anyone before in his rôle of sheep-killer, and he did not know what to expect. But when he saw the eyes of the man who was there to catch him, and the guilt and cowardice in those eyes, he, too, bowed his head, and the same look stole into his own eyes.

"Well," said the Master of Pen y Bryn weakly, when he could compose himself sufficiently, "Rover, old boy, so it's you, is it?" Rover came to him and licked his hand; at that moment a vague conflict was forming in the heart of the Master of Pen y Bryn, which he did not understand for a long time afterwards. But he did understand — eventually.

He sat on the heather without knowing how long, with

Rover guiltily licking his hand and alternately gazing into his eyes. Then it dawned on him that it would be best for him and Rover to go home as soon as they could, if they wanted to keep their secret; for he knew instinctively that if they arrived home safely the secret would be theirs for evermore. A dog caught doing such a thing once will never do it again.

On the way home, they heard someone coming to meet them, but before they could go and hide they ran into David Hughes the carpenter. He turned back with them, and the Master of Pen y Bryn told him that he had seen a slaughtered lamb, but despite a careful search he and Rover could not trace the killer. As they walked along, chatting pleasantly, David Hughes said: "I saw a funny thing on my way here. Old Jane Dodd was being walked up and down by old Robert and Matilda their daughter; she took an overdose of laudanum, they say, and they've got to walk her all night and give her some strong coffee every hour or so, in case she sleeps herself to death." They both laughed at this. David Hughes was more amiable than usual, and when they had walked a little further he suggested that they should have a smoke. They pulled out their pipes; David Hughes lit up and held out the match to the Master of Pen y Bryn, who brought his pipe up to it and prepared to shield the flame with his hands.

"Hello," said David Hughes, holding the match near his companion's hand, "why have you got blood on your hand, John Williams?"

The Master of Pen y Bryn pulled his hand back sharply, and Rover jumped up to it, thinking that he was holding something up for him; as he jumped he came into the light.

"Hey!" said David Hughes, "there's some blood on Rover's jaws, too: what's the meaning of this?" It was quite obvious, from his way of asking, that he understood full well. The Master of Pen y Bryn slipped his pipe into his pocket, grasped David Hughes' hand with both of his, and said entreatingly: "For God's sake, David Hughes, don't tell anyone. The killing is finished for good tonight, for good — please, David Hughes, don't."

"So it's all clear now," said David Hughes. "He was faithful to his partner in crime till the other came to kill your sheep, then he attacked him. I suppose the same thing would have happened if Rover had gone for the Foty's sheep, but then Shep would have been the hero, not Rover."

The Master of Pen y Bryn could say nothing but: "Don't tell, my dear David Hughes; please, don't tell; don't, David Hughes."

"On one condition," said David Hughes. "Do you remember asking me for advice some time ago?"

"Yes," said the Master of Pen y Bryn, his voice trembling.

"I haven't had the chance to give it to you before now," said David Hughes. "The condition is that you accept my advice."

"What is it?" whispered the Master of Pen y Bryn.

"I'll call round one evening, and give it to you," said David Hughes. "Well — we're almost at Pen y Bryn. Good night."

And off he went. In one single moment he had been transformed, in the eyes of the Master of Pen y Bryn, from a gentle person to a cunning, cruel one.

When he had gone the Master of Pen y Bryn turned towards the house; he bathed Rover's jaws in a nearby stream and went to chain him up. The collar was near the chain, done up. "He must have slipped his collar," he thought, and picked it up. But looking at the collar he found it was fastened by a different hole from the usual one — a different hole from the one he used when he tied Rover up the night before. That he was quite sure of. He put it round Rover's neck again and went indoors, his heart heavy as lead, wondering who could have let Rover loose to disgrace the family in this way. He decided that it would be best to reveal the secret himself, rather than let David Hughes give him away; but he thought it would be wiser to say nothing before he knew what David Hughes had up his sleeve.

Chapter XII

Cawgen Lake was round and deep, and there were lofty hedges around it; it was encircled by trees, so densely packed together that its waters were pitch black, even in broad daylight. The highway ran along one side of the lake and through the trees along the river; on the other side was a footpath which led nowhere except to the depths of the forest and an old, fallen tree trunk. It was so secluded that every timid creature fled there for shelter. There, you could see squirrels playing together, leaping from branch to branch like flying birds. It was there that every wounded bird nested and found a haven. And it was there, along the path which led to the heart of the forest, that lovers of seventeen or eighteen years old would go for a walk towards evening. The lake was so still, and the river so quiet, in this spot, that you could hear the tiniest bird shaking its wing, and the lightest of squirrels rustling the leaves as it sprang.

Knowing all this, it was not all courting couples that came to the place, although it was so shady; it was the youngsters who came. They came because it was, indeed, a very secluded place, but lonely as it was the old stagers knew that there were even better spots, places where the stones and the trees had not learned to listen or give away secrets. This element in the place brought the young louts here, too, who were too rough or too stupid to have girlfriends themselves. They came to lurk and to listen to young hearts brimming over, and got a sort of bestial thrill out of it.

One evening, the night when David Hughes the carpenter and the Master of Pen y Bryn were to go and watch the sheep, these youths heard a story they did not understand. From the depths of the wood, in the direction of the old tree stump, came the sound of light laughter which one could have mistaken for bubbling water, except that bubbling water did not exist there. Following the laughter, a girl's voice was heard saying; "Old David's as dry as dust today; I'm sure he was never young." Her companion laughed as lightly as she, and said, trying to be witty: "It's as if he had been born an old man." The effort may have been a failure, but to those carefree hearts who thought of nothing but their own ecstatic world, it was a great success, and they both had a hearty laugh at the words.

Emboldened by his success, the boy friend ventured on a more rash phrase, and said: "What was the old stick doing when you started out?" She greatly enjoyed the expression "old stick", and laughed at it a lot; and when she had regained composure she said: "He had his nose in the fire, looking as if the world were at an end, and everyone was doomed — and at this time of the year, too."

And that was how David Hughes' maid left him that night when she started out to meet her lover on the path near Cawgen Lake; with his nose in the fire, looking as if the world had come to an end and everybody was doomed. And since that image of him was so different from usual, the youths could not imagine who was being discussed or who was talking.

The locals never imagined that David Hughes could be depressed under any circumstances; nobody thought he was subject to what are termed emotions, much less that they could possibly get the better of him. He was, to the neighbourhood, common sense incarnate; and it was of that aspect of him which they spoke in chapel and market, in committee and council, whenever his name came up: on Sundays, holidays and workdays. He never gave any sign that there was another side to his nature. He never wept, however moving the sermon; even though the preacher might be standing on the brink of the grave, as it were, throughout the service, describing adults and children dying in ecstasy, enough to satisfy the most morbid of tastes. He did not laugh, however uproarious the fun. The best he could manage was a wintry greyness, or a bright, cold smile like the moon's, on such occasions. When he prayed on his knees, he put his case before the Almighty rationally and grammatically. His needs were always practical ones, and he never asked for anything he could not make full use of if he got it. For that reason, one never heard him ask for the great showers and the mighty outpourings.

He was a bachelor, and was remembered as such by the older generation, even by people older than he — he was a bachelor as a child. He wore a collar, and brushed his hair back like a man, before other children of his age had lost interest in muddy pools or got over their hatred of soap and water. He began to take a prominent part in chapel life and to read "The Pilgrim's Progress" while he was still young, and no one ever heard his voice tremble or his eloquence diminish.

Gradually, he became the neighbourhood's chief adviser. No lad would take over a farm, or buy a piece of land, or dream of starting life, without half an hour's tête-à-tête with David Hughes. When a man suffered bereavement or disaster he came to David Hughes for help and comfort, and if anyone needed to borrow money it was to David Hughes that he came. If he did not have any to lend himself, he knew someone who had, for there was hardly anyone who had not revealed his secrets to him at some time or another. His advice was always forthcoming, his eloquence flawless. And although the man who spoke to him might be so overcome with sorrow that he could hardly utter a word for tears, David Hughes spoke quite smoothly, and there was not the slightest tremor in his voice; and the other would feel himself sheltered by an immovable rock.

In this way he became the axis of local life. It revolved around him; many people felt that society would crumble if he went away. His smile was sunshine, his frown foggy blackness, in the eyes of the recipient. He had only been defied once, and that was at night, near the window of Tu Hwnt i'r Afon; and no one heard that defiant challenge but Mary, the daughter of the house, and David Hughes himself. He knew that his challenger was too brave to tell anyone about the incident, and he would not dream of doing so himself; and even if he had known that Mary had heard, he was astute enough to know that she would be too frightened to say anything. And David Hughes continued to move in society, as self-possessed as ever. When the tithe war came, everyone knew he would do the most prudent thing; and many people imitated him so that they might be considered prudent.

This was the type of man David Hughes was, to everyone almost without exception. He lived alone, and at first an old lady kept house for him. She had been with him for many years, so that she seemed a part of his possessions, but in the end she had to go the way of all flesh. He got a young girl in her place, the type whom they call "a flighty piece" and "an old bag" alternately. You could not imagine, in the eyes of the neighbourhood, two more different people living under the same roof, and this was what the girl felt, too. She sat on the tree stump that night, with her lover, having left her master gazing drily into the fire. But David Hughes himself, the wise man who would never descend to any tomfoolery, and who was immune from the frailties of human nature, had done the same thing once, and at the same time and place, just like his maid.

He, too, had been eighteen once, and at that time he had had a great spiritual awakening; and his soul had great depth, when it was awakened. But he had such self-control that only one person had ever had the opportunity to see the swelling of the great depths. She was like a gull on the surface of the wave; she could not feel the movement, because she was elevated by it, drawn into its swelling harmony, without herself contributing anything to it. He thought she had profundity of soul, too, so he was content to let depth call unto depth, thinking that the other would recognize the call; and here he failed. She could sing quite nicely, and he misunderstood her song for the language of her soul; but she was content just with the singing, without applying it to any other concept outside itself. And in those moments, looking at the soot playing on the bars of the grate, and listening to his maid's footsteps walking away from the house, his mind wandered over the path she trod, and he saw in the fire a familiar sight that he had seen there a hundred times before. He was a young man treading the same path, the maiden of his dreams beside him. He could see them meeting at that spot where the maid and her lover met; then they walked arm in arm through the wood towards the tree stump; and he took note of that part of his sleeve which her fingers had touched, so that he could lay his own fingers on the spot when he went back to his room.

He gazed deep into her eyes, and thought they had great depth. He asked her to sing to him, and she sang local songs — though, from her lips, they seemed new and fresh to him. There was one song he thought he would never tire of listening to her singing: "Y, deryn pur a'r adain las," "the gentle bird with the blue wing," and after leaving her, he did everything to the accompaniment of that song. He would find himself washing in the morning and moving his hands to the timing of "the gentle bird"; he sawed wood and planed wood to this accompaniment, so that his whole life was one song, and that song was "The gentle bird".

He did not impose any kind of conditions on her; he could not imagine that they would ever part. He thought that each was dependent on the other for harmony in life. He remembered how they walked along that path one evening to the old tree stump, and stayed there a long time. He was dreaming, gazing at her, and she was darting uneasy little glances in all directions. He thought her nervousness was caused by the passion in her heart. In his dream, he asked himself whether, perhaps, her life had another aspect to it; did she eat, drink and sleep like other mortals, or was she some kind of butterfly? Had her ears ever listened to the things human beings were usually compelled to listen to, or did she live on song, her thoughts filled only with the ideas expressed in her songs? He awoke from his dream to find her looking uncomfortable, as if she had hit on something she could not understand; but it was him she was looking at, and he thought her profound soul understood his soul to its greatest depths.

They started walking up a little hill away from the tree trunk, and got to the top just as the last rim of sun was slipping over the horizon behind the church. The scene which lay before them was enough to stir the meanest soul. The long plain stretched out below them, its borders lost in a light layer of mist; they could see the old church, almost from its foundations upwards, between them and the sky. Behind it, the sky seemed to be ablaze, burning with a red fire without a flame, and generating the most extreme heat; a deep murmur, which impregnated the silence with passion, came from the direction of the church as from the heart of some red-hot planet beyond the church and the horizon. You could see the rosy glow round the church and through the windows, particularly through the windows nearest the altar. David Hughes had been transported, through that scene, to a world in harmony with the tumult in his soul, and he turned to look at her. But she was scraping a spot of mud off the tip of her shoe, which had got there when she was climbing the hill. A shadow passed over his face for an instant, but a cloud could not survive for long in such heat, and his eyes shone like the church windows.

He pointed towards the scene, and said: "Jenny, there is my soul; the temple of my heart is ablaze tonight, and it is the altar which feels the heat most strongly." "Yes, it's nice, isn't it?" said Jenny, and went on scraping at the mud. He fell silent with a kind of half-sigh; he felt his soul shrivelling up inside him, and he turned away from her to gaze at the scene. As the fire sank and darkened, he felt the fire sinking and darkening in his bosom, but he soon came to when he heard her singing lightly at his side. He explained her behaviour as something to do with that element, strange to every man, in the nature of every female. They went back down the hill, and parted in ecstatic mood, after arranging to meet again.

She did not meet him next time as she had promised, and some time elapsed, during which he could not find her anywhere; and an unpleasant rumour circulated in the neighbourhood. No one knew that there was anything between him and the girl, so people had no hesitation in repeating the story in the carpenter's workshop, without glossing over any details to save his feelings. They said that she was going to be the Mistress of Y Ddôl, and the bitter details were trotted out in the expectation that he would laugh; he did not, so they thought the whole thing was just not his style, that it was too commonplace. He was so self-controlled that his face did not even begin to betray the laceration of his heart.

As he thought about the affair, in the lonely night, he remembered how she had behaved in one of the greatest moments of his life, and he saw it was not she that he loved, but a girl of his own creation. Whereupon a strange thing happened. The two became wholly separated in his consciousness — the girl, and the girl he used to think she was; the split was so definite that they became two different people. He left one to the Master of Y Ddôl, who became, in later years, the Master of Pen y Bryn, and kept the other for himself; it was in her company that he spent his leisure hours. He could find her whenever he pleased, for his heart was her home; she was his creation. She had never ventured from his heart into the cold world, and it was to her that he fled in those moments, when his maid was out walking with her lover near Cawgen lake. He had met Jane Williams hundreds of times since, and he was on perfectly good terms with her, but he was not at all jealous of the Master of Pen y Bryn for having married her, for she was not his love, but another woman, whom he once mistook her for; and the Master of Pen y Bryn could not take that one away from him. But if the Master of Pen y Bryn had failed to take his goddess from him, it was he that had shattered his image of her, and he would not blame himself much if he shattered some image cherished by the Master of Pen y Bryn, if ever he got the chance.

Experience taught him that Jane Williams had a small, kind, superficial soul, and that she just thought of those past encounters as simply "going for a walk" to wait till a big "catch" came, and he was no catch in those days. Gradually, he got to thinking that there was no place in the world for the girl of his imagination, and he kept her more tightly locked up in his heart than ever; and he just revealed to the world that aspect of himself which the world could understand. As he became more and more involved with the world, and gradually made money, his reputation and his influence grew, but he knew, through it all, that he was degenerating, and in his hours of solitude he sought the company of his ideal woman, lest he should lose his grip on the world she came from, the world he, too, lived in when he was eighteen.

Sometimes, he had a deep yearning for a real, living, talking version of that girl, and his soul longed for a companion, but he could not risk a second disappointment. He clung more closely to his brother as a kind of compensation, and when he saw him settled happily in his own home he amused himself by helping him; but that was not enough. David Hughes sighed at this point in his reverie, and he was frightened by the echo of his own sigh.

He leapt to his feet and walked round the house, regaining his sense of practical reality quickly enough to answer a knock on the door. He opened it and saw a man who had called on him that afternoon, enquiring about a coffin for his brother. David Hughes put on his special funereal expression, asked him in, and told him that he was expecting the wood any minute; he would start on the work as soon as it arrived. The man went away.

David Hughes remembered that he had promised to keep watch that night with the Master of Pen y Bryn. He sat down again, and tried to solve the riddle of the dogs. He went on to try and solve another one — how the Master of Pen y Bryn had managed to regain his farm when the estate supervisor had promised it to him for his brother; he had given the supervisor a hand-out on the side for his trouble. He decided he would see the supervisor again without delay. His mind revolved round these problems, like a moth flying from one candle to another.

"The other dog must have been Rover," he said. "Otherwise, how did Shep dare to come to Pen y Bryn at all, if he didn't expect a better welcome than he actually got?" He thought and hesitated, but in vain. "Tonight," he said, "I shall know once andfor all, and that will help to solve the other problem." Upon which the wood for the coffin arrived. David Hughes sent the maid, when she came in, straight to get the workmen to make the coffin; and then he sent her to tell the Master of Pen y Bryn that he could not accompany him at the appointed time, if at all.

He put the men to work. He stayed with them till he was sure that the Master of Pen y Bryn had set out for the mountain, then he went out for a walk. Soon he made for Pen y Bryn, and having made sure that everything was quiet and that everyone was asleep, he went to Rover and set him loose. He fastened the collar again — just as it was, or so he thought — and returned to the workmen. He stayed around for a while, then followed the Master of Pen y Bryn to the mountain. When he returned, he had the Master of Pen y Bryn where he wanted him.

Chapter XIII

The Master of Pen y Bryn stood on his threshold one evening, a couple of days after David Hughes, the carpenter, had threatened him. He was thinking of this and that at the time, and listening to a blackbird singing on the topmost branch of one of the poplar trees in front of the door. He enjoyed the blackbird's song, and at that moment he wished he could change places with it. Rover barked in the yard; the blackbird stopped singing for a moment and listened, then flew away towards the mountain. The Master of Pen y Bryn followed it with his gaze; he saw a hawk descending like an arrow from a bow, heard a screech, and saw black feathers flying in all directions; and he no longer wanted to change places with a blackbird.

It was fellowship meeting night, and almost time to go; and he concentrated, next, on the problem of whether it would be fitting to go there. He sang a hymn to himself, and described to himself the meeting and its speakers, just as he expected them to be if he went. Eventually, he imagined himself near to the corner of the pew next to the big pew, listening to the man who was sitting there getting up and telling of his experience. A shiver passed through him, and he looked fearfully towards the mountain, at the black feathers which were still rising anf falling on the breeze. "Why didn't he come the night before last?" he said to himself, "if he wanted to advise me; and he didn't come last night, either. I shan't let him tell anyone about Rover — I'll tell them myself first." His mind wandered to the sheep-watching and how he caught Rover, and how David Hughes caught both of them. The frightful shiver passed through him again, and he forgot the fellowship meeting in trying to decide why David Hughes had still not been to advise him. And when he had resolved, for a second time, to reveal Rover's secret rather than let David Hughes do so, an indefinable terror, quite beyond his comprehension, swept over him. Did David Hughes have some ulterior motive for delay? There must be some explanation, he was sure; it was on the tip of his tongue, as it were, but it vanished before he could grasp it and explain it clearly. Actually, the explanation was a very simple one. He remembered the fellowship meeting, and decided to go, if only to come to better terms with himself; for the adulation of the neighbourhood, and its effect on him, had begun to lose its piquancy and savour. The old restlessness was gnawing at him again, he felt, and stirring up other things in its wake. He was afraid of seeing the ghost of Mally Francis shedding her glory again, as she had done on that strange night which cost him so much pain. It was all this that made him decide to go to the fellowship meeting.

Suddenly, he saw Shôn Bach tiptoeing past the cowsheds and the barn, down to the hedge that encircled the field below the house. He gazed around him from time to time, to see if anyone was watching; so the Master of Pen y Bryn hid behind one of the poplars. Shôn Bach bent down when the hedge was low, and bent double when he passed a gap; he was grinning all the time. Rover barked at Shôn; Shôn raised his fist angrily at him, without knowing that his master was in sight. Rover followed him, his tail between his legs and his head held low, and Shôn himself went on walking like a cat stepping on embers. His master's curiosity was fully aroused now, and watching his youngest labourer and his dog made him forget about the meeting. In a few moments he saw his chief labourer coming from the direction of the stable, all bent, and walking just the same as Shôn Bach. He followed him, lurking in the shadow of the hedge, with a rather dubious expression, as if he could not quite understand what the young manservant was up to. The

Master of Pen y Bryn grew more bewildered still. When the chief labourer had passed the corner of the barn the Master saw Mary Eliza coming from the dairy, looking round her in case someone was watching; then she followed the men, going through exactly the same motions and gestures. When Mary Eliza had gone round the corner of the hedge that bordered the field below the house, her master heard the light crack of a thin branch. He went down to the corner of the barn and peeped round it. He saw Shôn going through a gap in the hedge into the field, then crawling on his hands and knees along a dried-up ditch; his grin was so wide you could see it for miles. The chief labourer followed him through the hedge, and went after Shôn on his hands and knees along the ditch. He, too, had a knowing smile on his face by now. Rover trotted lightly between them, wagging his tail, just as fascinated as the rest. Then he saw Mary Eliza crawling along the ditch after them; all four seemed equally keen on arriving somewhere pretty smartly, and getting a bit of entertainment.

No doubt they all thought their master was safely tucked away in the fellowship meeting. This was too much for the Master of Pen y Bryn, and he found himself sneaking furtively in the shadow of the barn and heading in the same direction as his servants. He, too, was smiling broadly; he did not know why, except that his manservants and his maid were grinning too. He got to the gap they had gone through. He hesitated a moment, wondering whether to go past it, but he went on to the other side of the field, opposite the others. He found a likely spot in the hedge and peered through it.

He saw a strange scene, and heard yells of enthusiasm at the far end of the field. He went down the road, near enough to the creature who was performing his antics there to recognize him and understand what he was saying. The first words he heard were: "Come on Hugh, come on Hughie; hey, Hugh, hey, Hughie." Then the strange creature jumped on to the wall, yelling: "Hoolay! Hoolay! Hugh best! Hugh best!" Meaning that Hugh was the victor in the contest; but where was Hughie? There was only one visible competitor and possible winner.

The Master of Pen y Bryn could see the heads of his manservants and his maid rising above the hedge from time to time, in the distance, and they seemed to be laughing uncontrollably. He laughed himself at the sight, but he still did not get the message; however, it was not long before he did. The sportsman was Hugh, Pant yr Afon, and he was running a race against himself. Hugh apparently got the idea sometimes that he was a dual personality; he called one side of him Hughie and the other Hugh. He made them both compete in various sports, and he himself, after the fray, was always on the winning side. The servants and maids of Pen y Bryn, and all the servants and maids and children in the neighbourhood, for that matter, knew all about this performance that Hugh used to put on. On this particular evening, Hugh and Hughie had got it into their heads to run a race. The dual personality stood stock still in the middle of the field, his feet together. "One, two, thlee," he counted, and off he went. But in two seconds he was back at the starting point. Apparently Hughie had started in front of Hugh.

The schizoid gentleman decided that the next competition would be to decide which could stand on his head the longest, Hughie or Hugh. They were to compete together, not in turn. They stood on their head till the face seemed about to explode, and their eyes looked like eggs, but neither would give in, and the distant audience could hear a shouting which was half encouragement and half groaning: "Go on Hughie, go on Hugh." Then there was a heavy sigh and a fall; both feet reached the ground almost at the same time. Then there was a big argument between the two contestants as to who stood on his head the longest. It developed into a quarrel. The quarrel went something like this: "Hugh won, no Hughie, no Hugh, no Hughie, no lad, Hugh, no my lad, Hughie; you pay me, lad, no, you pay me." One of them stretched out his hand and touched the air lightly, as if he were striking some object in front of him. The other came back with a harder punch; it was obvious that it *was* the other, because the fellow was standing in different places as he struck the two blows. The fighters threw off their coats, rolled up their sleeves, and set to. The contest was so fast and furious that, in the eyes of the beholders, the two figures melted into one, and the one was lashing out at the air. The boxers carried on in this way for a while and then sat down; the pugnacious expression gradually vanished from their face just like a rain cloud from the sky. Obviously, the prize had been divided. The next item was a stone-throwing competition, but a tragedy happened. Part of the river bank gave way beneath the competitors because, in their enthusiasm, they had unknowingly ventured too near the river. They fell flat on their face into the water, but their left foot got caught in the bank, so that it escaped having an involuntary bath. The contestants jumped up and got on to dry land, dripping from head to toe — with the exception, that is, of the left foot; but they were sporting enough to laugh. Hugh was laughing at Hughie because he had fallen into the river.

The Master of Pen y Bryn was enjoying the entertainment greatly. But then he felt something cold snuggling into his hand. He wheeled round and saw Rover gazing into his eyes with mingled entreaty and guilt. The dog was trying to squeeze himself between the man and the hedge, and kept looking back between whiles. His master raised his eyes to the direction his dog was gazing in. David Hughes, the carpenter, was standing about twenty yards away from him; he had obviously witnessed some of the fun at least. The Master of Pen y Bryn saw him, and gazed at him without a word.

"I see," said David Hughes, coming towards him. "So this is where you are, a sensible man like you — instead of coming to the meeting you're amusing yourself watching a half-wit trying to split himself in two."

"Yes, here I am," said the Master of Pen y Bryn; he had nothing else to say. He tried to hide the fact that he was trembling.

"Poor Hugh isn't the only dual personality in this world," said David Hughes. "But there's a difference. He's really only one, and even the one isn't all there, but he thinks there are two of him. Whereas some people have a dual personality and they try to give the impression that they're just one person."

"What do you mean, David Hughes?" asked the Master of Pen y Bryn.

"Did you tell people that Rover was the sheep-killer?" asked David Hughes.

"No," said the Master of Pen y Bryn, hanging his head.

"What I mean is," said David Hughes, "some people have dual personalities. Sometimes, for instance, you have a coward and a hero trying to co-exist."

The Master of Pen y Bryn cringed, as if someone had stabbed him, but he did not say a word.

"Are you sure you want to keep the secret about this being the sheep-killer?" asked David Hughes. And Rover squeezed himself more tightly between his master's legs and the hedge, and hung his head.

"Yes," said the Master, "if you are. I was just waiting till I saw you; but if you want the thing to come out, I'll tell people about it myself — to stop you slandering me."

"Too late," said David Hughes. "What will people say if you let the cat out of the bag now, after keeping mum for three whole days? Won't they get an inkling of what sort of man you really are?"

The Master of Pen y Bryn cringed again, and was silent. He could now understand, quite clearly, why David Hughes kept away for three days without coming to tender his advice — the reason had been on the tip of his tongue when he was standing on the doorstep, but it had escaped him. He tried to pull himself together. He stood up and looked David Hughes straight in the eye.

"What is your advice, David Hughes?" he asked. "So much depends on that advice."

"What was it you asked of me at the beginning of winter?" asked David Hughes.

"Advice about giving up farming," said the Master of Pen y Bryn, wondering what was coming. His courage was beginning to ebb.

"Well, that's it exactly," said David Hughes. "That's my advice."

"What?" The Master of Pen y Bryn was stupefied.

"Give up farming, as you said, next May Day," said David Hughes.

The Master of Pen y Bryn felt the anger rising in him. Like many cowards, he mustered up all his strength for one mighty effort to escape the talons of his opponent, and be free of the struggle.

"David Hughes," he said, "I don't want to leave the farm; you can do your worst. I'll tell them myself that Rover was the sheep-killer; I'll find some excuse for waiting three days, don't you worry." He now felt heroic enough to draw himself to his full height and flash his eyes as he delivered the challenge. His bluff was so effective that Rover, too, began to growl. David Hughes smiled nonchalantly and said:

"Well done, my hero. That's Hugh. Now for Hughie; it was he that got wet, wasn't it? Do you still think it's right not to pay the tithe?"

"Yes," the other said, "and since you talk of heroism, you'd be more of a hero if you did the same."

"Which is the more heroic," said David Hughes, "to pay the tithe and keep quiet about it, or not to pay it, get honour and glory heaped on you, and then slink off to the bishop to say you're sorry?"

The Master of Pen y Bryn grew pale as a sheet; the stick he was carrying fell to the ground and he trembled like a leaf. He tried to speak, but his throat was dry, and his words stuck to his palate. He visualized himself in the presence of the bishop, and in the light of David Hughes' merciless description he saw how disgusting the action had been. He repented with all his heart, but it was fear that dictated that repentance. This was the second time he had felt the ruthless influence of that particular dictator. David Hughes could see the conflict raging inside him. He grimaced contemptuously and drawled softly: "Hugh and Hughie again! What is going to fall in the river"? And who will have the laugh that time? Will it be Hugh? Will the hero laugh when he sees the hypocrite lying in the ditch?"

His bluff had been called; David Hughes had just laughed in his face. Would entreaty work, then?

"What have I done to you, David Hughes," asked the Master of Pen y Bryn, his voice drowned in tears, "to make you persecute me like this?"

"What have I done to *you*," said David Hughes, "that you refuse to take my advice after asking for it?"

"Who told you what happened between me and the bishop?" asked the Master of Pen y Bryn.

"Is it true?" asked David Hughes. "If it's true, no matter who said it. It's the message that counts, not the messenger."

"You hadn't even thought of such a thing three days ago," said the Master of Pen y Bryn, "or you would certainly have mentioned it."

"Many a big ship has been sunk; many battles have been won; and the fate of many nations, not to mention individuals, has been determined in less than three days," said David Hughes. "John Williams," he said again, drawing himself up, "let's give up the playacting. I'd better be straight with you. You know why you're being left sitting pretty at Pen y Bryn, unlike the others who refused to pay the tithe. It's because you begged the bishop for his forgiveness and licked the dirt off his boots. Then you came home, knowing that you had a comfortable hearth waiting for you — plus the undeserved adulation of innocent people who regard a hero as a kind of semi-god. Good Heavens, man! How can you live with yourself, knowing that you're such a humbug? Consider the matter in the light of your own conscience, instead of in the light of other people's opinions. Has it never dawned on you that there is such a thing as conscience? Or are you completely obsessed with using everything to your own advantage?"

"Why are you so anxious for me to move from Pen y Bryn?" asked the other. He felt like a limp rag in the presence of this strong man.

"That's not important," said David Hughes. "But justice demands that you should be shown up in your true colours. If you don't give notice to quit by New Year's Day, the whole neighbourhood shall be told what sort of hero you are." It did not occur to the Master of Pen y Bryn that David Hughes, in this respect, was disloyal to the cause of justice, since he was willing, under certain conditions, to suppress the truth. He stood there mutely, a picture of misery, and gazed at his opponent. David Hughes gazed past him at the sun setting over the church, and the church seemed about to burst into flame in the glow. He remembered a similar scene, many years ago; he had been thinking of it only the night before last. "No," he said to himself, "that shall not influence my relationship with this man in any way." Yet he pressed his lips more tightly together before he spoke again, and his eyes flashed with a more ruthless light. Both fell silent, gazing at each other, till they heard footsteps approaching from the distance.

"John Williams," said David Hughes, "here's my advice, and I expect you to take it between now and the end of the month. Some time ago, you considered giving up farming. Well, that's the wisest thing you can do. You have enough to live on, and if you don't make up your mind to do it by the end of the month, the locals shall know what sort of man they half worship — and you'll be despised more than you ever were."

As he was finishing the sentence, The Rev. T. Cefnllech Roberts came into view round the corner; he was on his way to Pen y Bryn for a smoke and a chat.

"How do you do, friends," he said, "who would have thought of finding you two nattering away here, instead of in the comfort of Pen y Bryn? Are you coming along?"

David Hughes was too wise, and too strong, to show that anything was wrong, and the Master of Pen y Bryn, too, tried to pull himself together as best he could. The three made for the house, for a chat and a smoke. The minister put as much life into the company as he could, but the conversation was extremely laboured, and he and David Hughes went off home pretty early, leaving the Master of Pen y Bryn to brood at home. On his way out David Hughes turned to the Master of Pen y Bryn and said: "Good night, John Williams; maybe we'll see more of Hughie and Hugh before long." Only the two of them understood the significance of this. On the way home the minister heard the story of Hugh and Hughie competing in the field, and he laughed heartily. He did not realise that a man who had been in his company a few minutes previously was being tormented by secret anxiety as he brooded on another angle of the same story.

The month that followed was a black one for David Hughes' prey. He had to keep the secret to himself, for his own sake; he could not even tell it to his beloved spouse, who was always so anxious to help him. He was sure that David Hughes would prove inflexible; so much so that within two days of the quarrel, the Master of Pen y Bryn and John Williams seemed an ocean apart in his estimation. The Master of Pen y Bryn was on a pedestal which the other could never aspire to; and he kept sinking lower and lower in his own eyes. His repentance, and his contempt for himself, engendered by the vision which David Hughes had brought before his eyes, were quite genuine. But as with all weaklings, the scale of his repentance and his self-hatred depended on the remoteness of his salvation. A weak man always blames himself, and quite conscientiously, when he has nothing to gain by blaming anyone else. The light of eternal judgement is the only light penetrating enough to reveal him to himself. So as his hopes of salvation grew more remote, his repentance and self-hatred grew, and he knew David Hughes well enough to realize that salvation was, indeed, very remote. He blamed himself for his weakness in going to ask for his advice in the first place, for the sole reason that he wanted to dramatize himself in his own eyes, and not for the advice itself. He thought of the way people changed their minds about him when he refused to pay the tithe, and he had lived in this new world of his so long that he had a holy terror of returning to his former state.

But now, he was in a much worse state than before. Whatever the locals had thought of John Williams before, they had never thought as little of him as John Williams now thought of himself. No matter what happened to distract his attention, his mind kept returning to the same old topic. David Hughes had a fatal attraction for him, as the north pole attracts the magnetic needle. His gaze always returned to him in chapel on a Sunday, and his mind wandered back to him constantly during the week. And every time this happened, he felt the blast of the cold north wind on his face. True, David Hughes' sense of justice was tinged with cruelty, but was not that true of divine justice, even? He had often heard tell of the wrath of God, and what was right in God must be right in man, after all. He brooded and cogitated, his mind wandering from this idea to that, like a bee going after honey, but he always came back to the same spot. The more he brooded, the more he longed to be an integrated personality, and the more he believed that David Hughes, after all, was right. He had been asking what David Hughes' motive could be for getting him out of Pen y Bryn, but now he was too full of repentance to worry about that. Whatever the reason, he was a hypocrite trying to look like a hero, and to remain the Master of Pen y Bryn, and he fully deserved his punishment. This he found easy to acknowledge, even in his most secret moments. This was the point he had reached within the month, and he kept muttering to himself: "John Williams and the Master of Pen y Bryn; Hughie and Hugh. Hugh laughed when Hughie fell in the water; who will laugh when John Williams falls in, I wonder?" And every time he asked himself this question, every instinct urged him to keep John Williams on dry land.

Chapter XIV

The month was up, and David Hughes the carpenter endeavoured, in every way he could, to find the Master of Pen y Bryn, to see if he was going to go along with his advice; but in vain. The sinner had repented, and acknowledged deep in his heart that the carpenter was right, and that he himself was completely unworthy of the status and respect he possessed; but it was extremely difficult to wait for David Hughes and admit all that to him, for the Master's perception was greater than his strength. David Hughes called at Pen y Bryn, but the master of the house was not in. He crossed over to him many times at the end of a fellowship meeting or a prayer meeting, but the object of his interest was invariably involved in a deep discussion with somebody or other, so much so that he never noticed that David Hughes was anxious to have an interesting and penetrating discussion with him. So a month, and five weeks, and six weeks, went by, till finally the time came to get the hay in, and everyone was full of fuss and bother. The neighbourhood was aroused by the sound of scythes and hay-cutting machines, and the shouting and chattering and laughing of the harvesters, and the sound of children jumping over the swathes of hay; vieing with each other to hold the horses' heads for the men with the machines and the whetstones for the men with the scythes, chasing corncrakes and looking for nests of field mice. It was such a pleasant season that the old became young again; you could see one or two of them hobbling along to this field and that, and sitting to watch the hay being cut, reminiscing about the wonderful way it was all done in the old days: how old so-and-so, who had been dead years, used to cut the hay in such and such a field in record time, and how it would still be like that if it were not for the mechanical harvester, which all the old people in the land regarded as their natural enemy. It had brought decadence and degeneracy to the rising generation, in their opinion. The arrival of the old folks calmed the children, because they enjoyed lounging about near them and listening to the strange stories about the supermen that inhabited the world before they entered it.

David Hughes knew it was no good looking for the Master of Pen y Bryn at the moment, because he was in the middle of harvest fever. But he was not worried: there was plenty of time to New Year's Day. Nevertheless, he would have been glad to feel certain in his mind that his brother would be in Pen y Bryn by May Day. Before long, something happened which, he felt, might be favourable to a meeting with the Master of Pen y Bryn. After a week's harvesting, there was a change in the weather. As the first loads of hay were being brought from the fields, there was a thunderstorm, and a whole week's work was ruined. Weeks of unsettled weather followed. Sometimes there would be a reasonable day, followed by one which destroyed all the work done on the good day.

One fine evening, after a rainy morning, David Hughes decided to call unexpectedly at Pen y Bryn, so that he could finally have a chat with the Master on the topic which was so vital to both. He was certain that his mission carried the seal of success: so much so that he hummed gently to himself as he got ready to go. His maid was so surprised to hear him, of all people, giving some sort of expression to his feelings, that she could not get on with her work. Between seven and eight he started out for Pen y Bryn through Pandy Wood, the nearest route. Pandy Wood was ancient, full of different kinds of trees, and the river was particularly lovely there. It had cut a deep bed for itself, and had carried the peaty water down from the mountain, so that the soil and the stones and the tree trunks were all the colour of peat; and the foam in those shadowy depths looked like wild flowers culled from exotic gardens in a foreign land, drifting down on the surface of the water. No one could look on that water, so different in hue from the streams that sprung in the nearby meadows, nor gaze at those flowers of foam, without being prey to certain strange emotions. One would be overcome with longing for a land one could flee to, through the portals of which no fear, no persecution and no anxiety could gain admittance. The trees leaned over that deep river bed — the oak, the alder, the ash, the maple, the poplar, the aspen — and the hazel trees intermingled with them. On this particular evening the aspen leaves and the poplar leaves were trembling, though there was no hint of a breeze; their rustle, and the murmur of the waters, were the only sounds in the wood, apart from the occasional rabbit fleeing from a creature that thirsted for its blood. On the fringe of the wood you could hear the cuckoo, the lapwing, the corncrake and the fieldfare, and occasionally a sheep bleating and her lamb answering. A soul bent on being miserable would find it hard to be self-possessed in this spot, and it was to this spot that David Hughes came on his way to Pen y Bryn to pronounce his verdict.

He was no sooner in the wood than he came across a pair of lovers whom he knew well; they walked past him. They were quite accustomed to courting; they had walked these paths together before many of today's lovers had been born, and the paths they trod were the same. David Hughes smiled as he passed the old couple, and it was a long time before his smile faded. He made his way onwards through the wood, but the magic of the place was too much for him, and he could not walk far without stopping to listen to the rustle of the trees and the murmur of the water, and the song of birds beyond. As he was standing in this way, he heard the crack of branches from the direction of the river, and he saw two other lovers leaning against a great oak above the river, half turned towards him; they were so engrossed in their mutual love that they were oblivious of the fact that someone could be watching.

"Wait a minute," said David Hughes. "Who are they, I wonder? That girl looks familiar somehow . . . Phew! It's close in this wood." Presently the couple moved away, and walked slowly, arm in arm, down the path leading to the river, and David Hughes found himself gliding from tree to tree after them. When the path reached the point immediately above the river, it stopped, and there was a sharp drop of two yards to a stone lying in the bed of the river, with a shady nook nearby. It was easy to climb down at that spot, using the roots of trees as convenient stepping stones; you could hold on to a supple branch which bent as you descended till you were standing safely on the stone. There was a bend in the river at this spot, and the sides of the river bed formed walls two or three yards high; the trees bent over to form a shady roof, and their roots, with the mud washed away, could be used to sit on, so that those who had retreated to the spot had a little room to themselves, far from the world's gaze. A few yards away, above the furthest part of the bend in the river, there was an old hollow oak tree behind some thorns and brambles; it was large enough for two corpulent men to go inside together, and there was a hole in it which formed when a withered branch fell away. This hollow tree was the only place you could watch the nook from, without letting the occupants of the nook know that anyone was watching.

The lovers whom David Hughes was watching reached the spot above the nook; he was still gliding from tree to tree in pursuit. "Confound it," he said, "I should recognise that girl, I really should," and he slipped behind a tree, closer to them. He kept getting closer to them until he was within a few yards of them as they stood above the river. Hardly anyone who knew him would have thought him capable of such an action; and it was an action unworthy of him. But when a man's mind is concentrated on an unworthy action, as his mind was that night, the moral temperature drops, as it were, as the temperature of the sea does when there is an iceberg; and other unworthy actions come naturally to him, which he would despise in his normal frame of mind.

"Upon my word," said David Hughes, "if it isn't the lad from Plas Isa who bought that little pony at Pen y Bryn auction." He drew still closer to them. The lad got hold of the branch that hung over the river, and glided smoothly on to the stone on the river bed. The girl, too, grasped the branch after him, and swung down just as gracefully as he. They both laughed lightly and walked along the water's edge till they came to the nook; and they sat on the root of a tree to watch the water. David Hughes recognised the girl's laugh; it was a similar laugh to the one he heard many years ago when his heart was light and full of hope, before the world had hemmed it in; and he began to feel uneasy. He slunk past the thorns and brambles to the hollow tree and went into it. He looked through the hole in the tree; the pair beneath him were directly in view. "Who would have thought it?" he asked himself. "That's Annie, Pen y Bryn. I never heard a word about it from anyone; neither did anyone else, I should imagine. That's why the lad bought the little pony — and that's why Annie wasn't heartbroken when she saw it go. The pair of them understood one another perfectly — young people are deep ones, aren't they? Isn't she like her mother when she was young? The spit and image, and her soul is the spit and image too, I suppose; a thimbleful of a soul. Old Pen y Bryn doesn't know about this, otherwise he wouldn't have told me that time that Annie had no desire to settle down — unless this is something more recent. He would retire tomorrow if he knew that Annie and the Plas Isa lad would settle in Pen y Bryn. I'd better watch my P's and Q's if I want brother Dick to have Pen y Bryn. Just you wait, John Williams; you'll be feeling pretty queer before you tumble into bed tonight."

This was David Hughes' monologue as he watched the lad from Plas Isa and Annie, the daughter of Pen y Bryn, through the hole in the hollow trunk. As he watched, he saw the couple hold hands, and whisper; and though you could hardly hear the murmur of the water, it was loud enough to drown their words. The Plas Isa boy took a stone and threw it into the water; and the murmur of the water acquired a charming tone as it bubbled over the stone. It was part laughter and part singing, and sometimes the laughter interrupted the singing, so abruptly that the couple themselves laughed to hear it. David Hughes perceived, sooner than he had expected, that he was on hallowed ground; he felt he had rushed in too clumsily and rudely when he came to this spot.

After listening for a long time to the laughter and the singing, and whispering intimate secrets, the Plas Isaf lad turned to Annie and said: "Annie, you sing." "What if someone hears and comes along here?" Annie said. "No fear," said the youth. "No one ever thought of coming to a place like this before." He climbed up the root-steps, looked about him to make sure, and went back down. Annie began to sing softly, hardly louder than the murmur of the water, if indeed it *was* any louder. As she sang her bosom heaved and her eyes shone; for Annie had profundity of soul, and that soul was aflame with the power of love. The Plas Isaf boy sat beside her, then he would get up and stand before her, and then sit down again; then he would get up a second time, his eyes like flames, and his flushed countenance denoting that an ocean of feeling was swelling in his breast.

Finally he sat beside her and grasped her hand, and gazed ecstatically at her; she went on singing softly, on and on, song after song. Finally she stopped, and they both stayed still and silent for a long time, without a sign of life apart from their flashing eyes and heaving breasts. David Hughes could not bring himself to leave the hollow tree, although he had been wanting to for some time. He recognised the voice; he had heard it from another years ago. But *her* eyes had not been aflame, and her breast did not swell, and she had no profundity or awareness of soul. He once thought she had, but experience over the years taught him that he had been mistaken, and it was only gradually that he learned to recognize profundity of soul when he met it. And this girl who stood in front of him had a great tempestuous soul behind those eyes and that voice. He regretted coming there; this was no place for him. Then the Plas Isaf youth turned to Annie and said: "One more song, Annie, before I go." "Which one?" Annie asked.

"Anything you like; everything you sing is all right with me," he said. He broke off an ivy leaf and gave it to her. Annie knew the significance of the ivy leaf, and she took it, her cheeks burning. She broke off a leaf and gave it to him, and she began to sing softly:

"Y deryn pur â'r adain las,
Bydd imi'n was dibrydar;
O! brysur brysia at y ferch
Lle rhois i'm serch yn gynnar."

In the magic of that singing she rose and faced her lover. As she faced him, she faced the follow tree, and David Hughes saw her, radiant with all the glory and beauty of a soul on fire. He almost swooned. He saw, standing before him, the girl he had always loved, the girl into whose company he had fled over the years when the world weighed heavily on him, and had too much attraction for him — lest it swallow him altogether. Here was the girl who had brought light to his life ever since he was a lad of eighteen, the girl he had lived for, worshipped and pursued from day to day and from year to year. She was the girl his heart's love had created, who dwelt in his heart, and who had never left his heart, up to now, for the cold air of the world; now, that girl was standing before him, in the flesh, for the first time ever. He regarded Annie's mother for years as the broken image of his goddess, but now the goddess herself had stepped out of his heart. He was gazing at her, face to face, here, for the first time. And David Hughes gazed at her like one possessed, throughout the whole song, and he went on gazing at the same spot after she had sat down again and after the two of them had got up and left. He stood there gazing, meditating, expecting to see the charming vision again; and he had never been so reluctant to leave any place as he was to leave the old hollow tree that night.

Yes, she was the very incarnation of the girl he had always loved, the girl no one knew existed, but who was in his heart for all that, for him to adore and to worship, and she to comfort him, and to keep his eyes fixed on the skies in spite of the strong temptation to gaze down at the earth. By now, his journey to that hollow tree had become a journey to the Land of the Fairies, who had cast a spell upon him. When he made a move it was dark, and he had to grope his way through the wood. He went back home: to think. He could not risk causing pain to a man who had under his roof a girl like the girl he saw on the river bank — not without weighing the matter up; particularly as it involved hurting her, too.

Hardly any of his acquaintances would have recognized him that night if they had met him; he walked so unsteadily, and he was mentally so confused. He went in, sent the maid to bed, and sat there without fire or light, to think and to talk to himself. If one put his thoughts into words, they would be something like this

"Well, he's her father, that's the trouble. If he left, she would have to leave too; and if he stayed on in disgrace after I'd exposed his falsehood, she would have to bear the disgrace all her life. If he doesn't leave, and I keep quiet, brother Dick is going to suffer; and he's getting on so well, too, and deserves a big farm. If I tell, she is going to suffer; and if I hurt her, I shall be the one to suffer most. If I hurt Annie, the girl in my heart will be murdered — sure enough; life won't be worth living after that. Heavens! what if I had exposed the Master of Pen y Bryn, and then found out what his daughter was like? I would have gone mad. I was on the edge of a precipice! How different she is from her mother! The same body, the same eyes, but not the same soul, and John Williams could not take that soul away from me when he took Jane Williams, because she hadn't one. But Annie has. She's the same, exactly the same, as this girl I have locked within me; but I had never seen her before going down to the riverside tonight. At last — she's alive, in the flesh. Yes, if I give Annie any pain, I'd kill that girl, and — God, what a world this would be then — black, dark, cloudy, and misty, like a scattered dawn on the mountain tops. Brother Dick, you'll have to stay at Y Ddôl for a little while yet. It will affect you rather badly. It would affect John Williams badly if he left Pen y Bryn or, what is worse, people got to know what he was really like; and it would affect Annie badly. But if I drive him away, or expose him, I shall be the worst affected: I shall see the destruction of someone within myself, someone who has always been my very cause for living. Annie is the incarnation of that being. There's no doubt that if I murdered her, tore her from within me, that would be the cardinal sin against the Holy Ghost, for me. No, I won't; that's a sin I'll never commit."

David Hughes was absolutely right in this. To destroy that image in his mind, the image that had maintained him in an integrated state throughout the years, and kept him on the right path despite many false steps — that would have been his sin against the Holy Ghost. This sin does not take the same form for everyone, but for everyone its essence is the same: the destruction of the embodied reality, created in the soul, of everything that is pure and exalted, the destruction of Him that stands high on the mountain, entreating, and saying: "Come up hither, and I will show thee." That night David Hughes, the carpenter, fought the great battle of his life, and won it. On the one side stood the most attractive material elements: revenge for hurt pride, the good of his won flesh and blood, and wordly success; on the other side stood an image, and nothing else, an image no one in the world knew existed but himself, and which no one would ever know about; but an image that symbolized, by its very being, all he had ever held sacred. And the image won.

He went to bed some time in the dead of night, feeling more youthful than he had felt for years; his soul was pure, the world at his feet. In the triumph of victory he experienced rebirth. He despised all the petty meannesses that he had ever cherished, and more than anything, the way he had persecuted that weak character, the Master of Pen y Bryn. He recognised that he was weak and that he, David Hughes, was strong; but was that not a reason for defending him and not persecuting him? David Hughes slept peacefully that night, having decided to leave John Williams in Pen y Bryn without disclosing the secret, and to leave it between him and his conscience, if he had one, as far as his double life was concerned. He awoke the next morning, and the glory of the woman his soul had created was more radiant than ever. The dawn of that glory shone on everything he possessed, and his joy was unbounded.

His relationship with the Master of Pen y Bryn became quite relaxed, and he decided not to speak to him till he met him accidentally. This happened one afternoon at the village fair. He knew he had been avoiding him all day; and at one point in the afternoon, when he was paying a call on the blacksmith, David Hughes was watching him through a niche in the wall of the smithy. John Williams was talking to Samuel Jones, Y Tŷ Glas; his expression was sombre, as if some burden were about to weigh him down. He looked uneasily over his shoulder now and then, and David Hughes knew he was watching him. He left the smithy and went over to him, laying his hand on his shoulder, and he told him he would like a word with him when he was through with Samuel Jones. The Master of Pen y Bryn looked at him as if he had just awoken to find the dawn of the last judgement shining on his face.

When he had finished with Samuel Jones he went to him; he could not do otherwise after such a definite request. David Hughes asked him if he had much to do in the village; that he could wait; the Master of Pen y Bryn assured him that he was about to set off home. They walked together to Pen y Bryn, chatting about this and that. When they were out of public view, and started going across the fields, David Hughes stopped and looked the Master of Pen y Bryn straight in the eye. The other looked back at him like a naughty child at his schoolmaster.

"John Williams," said David Hughes, "you know what I want of you."

"Yes," said John Williams, his voice trembling.

"Have you made up your mind?" asked David Hughes.

The Master of Pen y Bryn did not answer. He just stood there like a prisoner awaiting the death sentence.

"Well," said David Hughes, "*I* have made my mind up. As far as I am concerned, Rover's secret will remain between you and me for ever. And as far as I'm concerned, again, the way you licked the bishop's boots will be a secret for ever between you, the bishop, the steward and myself. It was the steward who told me. I won't try to drive you out of Pen y Bryn or slander you publicly. And it is that angelic daughter of yours, Annie, that you have to thank for it. She showed me the cast in my own eye, and I have got rid of that now. I can see my way to salvation clearly enough, and my salvation presupposes protection for you. That is why I feel I have received true salvation. Go and thank God, on your knees, for your daughter. She saved you without knowing. The essence of the matter is what she is, and not what she did; she knows nothing of her own heroism. Nevertheless, she is the atonement for your sins," and David Hughes' voice broke here, and he trembled all over, and the Master of Pen y Bryn saw, for the first time in his life, how much feeling he was capable of. David Hughes gave him his hand; they shook hands and he turned away without another word.

The Master of Pen y Bryn could not grasp at once what had happened to him. When he had worked things out pretty accurately, he did not sink to his knees, but spun round on his heels. He spun round three times, and danced and ran homewards like a madman, dancing and running in turns. His wife supposed, when he arrived, that he had had a drop too many, and this surprised her; for this was Llangeunant fair and not Llangain fair. That night, her husband was obsessed with Annie; Annie this and Annie that, till Annie herself began to think that there was something very wrong with her father. He walked all over the house and across the yard like a lad of eighteen, and would turn back from wherever he was every few seconds, to say something to, or about, Annie, and he could not stop smiling, even when he was talking seriously. He went to the fields to look at the state of his hay, and he stopped every now and then to look at his farm, and to spin round on his heels whenever he thought himself unobserved. "Annie," he said, "Annie, my daughter, achieved all this. What did she do I wonder? Never mind; everything is all right." And just like some village idiot who used to live in the neighbourhood, when he was very pleased, the Master of Pen y Bryn shook hands with himself.

He stood in the middle of the field and his mind encompassed his daughter's life story. He remembered the story of her birth, and that was anything but pleasant. Even so, it was *Annie* who was born, then. She had such a blaze of glory around her, for him, that the significance of that event had been transformed. "If it were not for that," he said, "Annie would not have been given to the world — or to me." And his sin, in his eyes, became a true contribution to life. It had brought an inherent blessing with it. And surely, this is one aspect of atonement — the transformation of the meaning of sin, making even sin a means of blessing for mankind, a blessing which would never have been available otherwise. His sin — indeed all his sins — took on a different guise for the Master of Pen y Bryn when he realised that Annie's virtues had saved him from the necessity of breaking up his home — or living under a cloud. "I shall continue to be the Master of Pen y Bryn for a while yet," he said, "because I'm Annie's father, however poor a speciment John Williams may be. But — is John Williams really a poor specimen? On second thoughts, he's not so bad. John Williams is Annie's father, not the Master of Pen y Bryn — yes, me, John Williams; and John Williams must be quite an admirable man to have produced such a daughter."

John Williams swelled with pride at this point, and realised that he was as good as the Mater of Pen y Bryn any day; his status conferred no honour on him and it was no come-down for the Master of Pen y Bryn to be united with John Williams. Whatever the neighbourhood thought of the Master of Pen y Bryn, Annie's father could live up to him—and he and his status became integrated in his eyes. For him, as well as for the neighbourhood, the Master of Pen y Bryn and John Williams were one and the same now. This integration was achieved, not through dragging the Master of Pen y Bryn down or casting a slur on his glory, but by elevation of John Williams. Annie's father was worthy of any honour.

John Williams was perfectly content with this mental unity between himself and his status.

Chapter XV

It was Christmas Eve. A layer of snow covered the surface of the earth, and there was a frosty tang in the air. That evening, just before the sun had completely set, Lewis, one of Mathew Thomas' sons from Y Pant, stood in front of the doctor's gate, hands in pockets. He was freezing in the cold and gossiping with Ned y Pentre, his face pale and his nose red. However much they laboured to keep the conversation going, the cold defeated them, and they were content with an occasional word here and there.

"Who did you say was sick at home?" asked Ned.

"My dad," said Lewis. He fell silent for a while.

"Very sick?" asked Ned.

"Yes, quite."

"What are you doing here?" said Ned by and by.

"Waiting for the doctor to get back from our house," said Ned, and the conversation reached deadlock again.

Suddenly, Lewis' face lit up, and he asked Ned eagerly.

"Will you come carol singing?"

Ned thought for a bit, then he said:

"All right, but I've only got two or three; how many have you got?"

"Something like that," said Lewis. "Do you know 'In the Waters' and 'The Prodigal Sons?"

"Of course," said Ned, and off they went; and the next thing you could hear was Ned and Lewis in the dusk singing carols outside people's doors. They sang:

"Blant afradlon, at eich Tad,
Mae i chwi groeso,
A fu 'mhell o dir eich gwlad
Yn hir grwydro,"

("Prodigal sons, your Father welcomes you,
You that have wandered long and far
From your native land").

This was not, it is true, very flattering on Christmas Eve, and their other choice was not very cheerful or appropriate either:

"Yn y dyfroedd mawr a'r tonnau,
Nid oes neb a ddeil fy mhen,
Ond fy annwyl briod Iesu
A fu farw are y pren."

("In the mighty waves and waters, there is no one to hold my head aloft,
But Jesus, my beloved, who died on the cross").

But they were religious verses, and that was enough for Lewis and Ned. The pair of them went from door to door, singing; sometimes they would get an apple, sometimes a halfpenny, or an orange, and occasionally a threat or a curse. When this last gift came their way, the songsters doubled their efforts, in order to convince this particular audience of its sinfulness and damnation. They were so successful that before long they had gathered together multitudes of children; singing throatily every hymn they had ever been taught; the ones just mentioned and this one for a climax:

"Wele'r dydd ofnadwy'n dyfod
I falurio'r ddaear ddrwg,
I lwyr losgi lloches pechod,
Wele'r mellt, y tân, a'r mwg."

("The day of dread is at hand; it will demolish the wicked earth, it will burn down the havens of sin. Behold the lightning, the fire, and the smoke").

Every child is an evangelist, and a formidable one.

Soon, there came the sound of a carriage, which Lewis

recognised as the doctor's, and he ran after it for medicaments for his father. He started off for home loaded with goodies; his pockets were crammed with apples, oranges and sweets, and threepence halfpenny besides. He had often thought of buying himself a pistol when he had enough money, but they cost sixpence halfpenny, except in a sale. He had a mental conflict about which he should buy with the threepence halfpenny, and in the end he decided to buy his father an ounce of tobacco, to help him get better. He bought the tobacco and then set off home, oblivious of the cold. The snow was falling more heavily as he climbed up towards Y Pant, and he was sweating.

When he was fairly near the house, he saw someone coming to meet him, a figure looming between him and the sky. It was the Rev. T. Cefnllech Roberts. The minister came to him, laid his hand on his head, looked strangely at him, and said, "Be a good boy, my boy — don't forget," and went on his way. Lewis squeezed the ounce of tobacco more tightly in his hand and decided that he was a good boy already. How could he give his father the tobacco without being seen? That was the big problem. He went into the house; a great silence reigned there. The children clustered around the bedroom door, looking scared, and Moses was holding them back. Every now and then the silence was broken by a half-frightened chatter. "My turn to look," one would say. "No, mine," said the other. The argument was — who should stick his head in to see his father next, and it was always Moses who made the momentous decision. Lewis realised, then, that things were not as they had been when he left home three hours ago. He rushed through the crowd of brothers into the bedroom and said: "Dad," but no one answered. He just caught a glimpse, instead, across the bed, of his mother's furrowed brow; her eyes were wet and shining. His father lay in bed, his face white as chalk, his radiant eyes looking at the ceiling; he had a smile on his face, and his hand, outside the bedclothes, was tightly clasped in that of his wife. Lewis slunk back furtively to his brothers and his sister, and once again fingered the tobacco in his pocket. He swore them all to secrecy, making them promise that they would not tell their grandmother, who was bent double over the fire, or their mother even; then he showed the children a corner of the tobacco packet, and whispered: "Dad." In that moment, they were all possessed of a great envy of Lewis, their brother. They stayed there for a long time — Moses was doorkeeper, letting them all in turn peep around the door occasionally, to get a glimpse of their father.

Complete darkness engulfed the house; but the children continued to stand near the bedroom door. The mother rose, meaning to go to them for a moment, but she felt the hand squeezing hers more tightly; and she saw her husband's lips moving. She bent down, and heard the words: "Sally — till the end — now." She called Moses to help her and asked him to light the candles and go and look for help; but she could see the sick man's lips moving again, whispering the same words, and the head shaking to indicate "no." Moses lit the candles in the bedroom and the house generally, and eventually he and Sarah Jane put the smallest children to bed and went to bed themselves.

The clock struck seven in the other room and went on ticking, ticking; it was the only sound in the room, apart from the sick man's laboured breathing. He was still looking upwards and smiling, and squeezing his wife's hand, so that she could not move from the spot. The silence deepened; there was not a sound anywhere; just the clock ticking and the sick man's quick breathing. The lips moved again. "Well, Mathew dear," his wife said, "what can I do for you?" He shook his head and the lips whispered: "Sally — to the end," and some other words she did not understand.

The clock struck eight and went on ticking, ticking; then a little squeak was heard from the direction of the door. The woman looked round, and saw the door slowly moving, as if a light breeze were opening it, but she could not see anyone. She happened to glance towards the bottom of the door, and saw a little hand grasping it; and there was Jimmy, on his knees, peeping round the lower edge of the door, trying to get a look at his father. He came in, looked at him, and rushed out. The children had been drawing lots in bed about going to see their father in turn, and they came one by one, barefoot, on their hands and knees. Lewis came in his turn, with his ounce of tobacco in his shirt sleeve. He peeped furtively round the door, and failed to make the return journey when the time came; the next one on the list was getting impatient in his bed. He opened the door wider, and slid in on his hands and knees. He pulled the packet out of his sleeve, showed the edge of it to his mother, pointed at his father and stage-whispered: "Carols." His mother understood, and the sick man felt something warm coming down on his hand. He moved his lips; his wife bent over him; and he heard a whisper: "Sally—to the end," and those other strange words. The clock struck nine.

The children fell asleep, one by one; all but Lewis. He slipped out of bed again, opened the bedroom door, and showed the ounce of tobacco to his mother again round the door, pointing to his father with it. She shook her head and turned to moisten her husband's lips. He whispered her name, and those other words she could not understand. She stayed there for an eternity, listening to the tick of the clock and her husband's breathing, and every other sound one can hear at the dead of night; from the sound of a fly on the wall to the distant murmur of Ceunant river at the bottom of the valley. The clock struck ten. She tried to pull her hand gently from her husband's grasp to go and call Moses, but he clung to it with a grip of steel. He whispered her name again, and that promise, and those other strange words.

She thought she heard a gentle tapping at the door, and she listened. She heard someone lifting the latch and coming into the house. The bedroom door opened slowly, and the Rev. T. Cefnllech Roberts thrust his head in. The Master of Pen y Bryn stood behind him. "So you're not too well, my dear Mathew Thomas," said the minister. The sick man smiled more happily than ever — and that was all. The minister sank to his knees at the foot of the bed and said a few words to him about the dark valley; but Mathew Thomas smiled more benevolently than ever at that. The minister talked about the Lord of the Great

Beyond, and Mathew Thomas went on smiling, as if he were listening to an old tale he understood perfectly. Presently, a tear streaked slowly down his face. The minister bent down towards his lips and heard him whispering: "Sally — to the end," and the other words.

"What was it you last said, my dear Mathew Thomas?" he asked. The lips moved again and the minister understood. "Yes, Mathew Thomas," he said. "Sally and the children, and Jesus, and Johnny. Your wife and children will be safe under the protection of Jesus," and the sick man smiled more than ever. His wife felt him pulling her hand towards him; she bent down, and this time she, too, understood. Mathew Thomas whispered those words again, closed his eyes and slackened his grip. The last word that passed his lips was the name of the year-old child whose death was the final seal on the union between him and his wife.

The Master of Pen y Bryn was quite overawed by all this. The minister called Moses, and sent him to fetch some help and company for his mother. The old lady, who had fallen asleep sitting on the wooden settle near the fire, woke up. When the woman who was to help arrived, the minister and the Master of Pen y Bryn set off for home. The former talked to his companion, but the other was silent; he walked on with his head down. They parted at the corner of the village, and the minister watched him walking homewards, like a somnambulist, till he disappeared from view.

When he had reached a little hill near the house, the Master of Pen y Bryn stopped and gazed on the valley below him, white in the snow and the moonlight. He looked upwards, and saw a very bright star directly in front of him. He leaned on a nearby gate and gazed at the stars, oblivious of the frosty tang in the air. "Mathew Thomas!" he whispered to himself, "Mathew Thomas Y Pant! Where is Mathew Thomas now? Is he up beyond that star, I wonder? Is he travelling, travelling all the while, past that one, and then far, far beyond it? And the stars are very far away, so David Hughes the carpenter said. Isn't it rather cold for him to travel all that distance? Where is

Mathew Thomas tonight, I wonder? He was smiling as he lay dying — and he was just Mathew Thomas, Y Pant. Y Pant has neither added to his status nor detracted from it. Mathew Thomas never passed me by without bowing. My world was a pretty elevated one as far as he was concerned; and yet he was smiling as he died — as he *died.* He is in a strange world tonight that I know nothing of, but he was smiling as he went there, as if he knew it well. Has he reached that star, I wonder?"

A party of carol singers came by and said good night to him; each one touched his cap. He watched them disappear from view, and started off for home. "They wouldn't bow to Mathew Thomas," he thought, "and yet Mathew Thomas was smiling as he died. The preacher last Sunday was talking about heaven as a nobleman's palace. Mathew Thomas didn't know much about noblemen, but he has seen the Palace and the Master of the House; yet he went to meet him smiling, not touching his cap as he did with me. Shall I be able to smile then, I wonder, as I go towards the Palace?"

At this point he got to the house, and Annie opened the door to him. The carol singers had reminded him of what the neighbourhood thought of him; and he could see in Annie that harmony which, through her, he had achieved in his own consciousness, between himself and his status in society. But how to explain this new burden that was being laid on him by the creation and its great mystery?

He told his wife about Mathew Thomas. "Heavens," she said, "I've been hearing a little bell tinkling in my ear for hours, and I thought that was what had happened. John, we'll go there at once." She filled a basket with Christmas treats and other necessities and dressed to go out, and the pair of them set off towards Y Pant. They got there pretty soon. They made straight for the kitchen fire. The mother and grandmother were in the corner by the fire, looking bewildered and numb. On the other side, almost hidden away in a corner, sat Lewis, in his nightshirt. Everyone had forgotten about him, so he had fallen asleep, leaning on the chimney nob, clasping the ounce of tobacco tightly in his hand; and the woman who had come to help was tidying up the house.

Jane Williams went over to Lewis and grasped the hand that held the tobacco. She started a conversation with him in order to hide her generous and tender emotions.

"What have you got there, Lewis my boy?" she asked.

He awoke rather flustered. "Dad," he said. Gradually, she got the story of the tobacco out of him. "Your father will never smoke again, dear," she said gently, laying her hand on his head, and Lewis slipped from her grasp to the children's room.

"Hey," he staged-whispered wildly in the ear of each child, "my father's dead." No one knew what that meant, but they all got up before they were properly awake, and clustered round their mother like birds flocking to the shleter of a tree from the storm—before the storm broke, and before they could understand it.

Mathew Thomas used to be a labourer at Pen Y Bryn, and the Master, in his great mercy, offered to pay all the funeral expenses, but Sarah Ann Thomas refused. He may have been a labourer at Pen y Bryn, but he was her husband, too, and she had to bless his coffin with her heart's blood. They were poor, very poor, and the Master of Pen y Bryn was amazed at this stubbornness. Neither he nor his wife could enter the world of Sarah Ann Thomas; the rich man cannot enter the world of the poor, even though the generosity of his heart be unbounded. Their separate worlds are as different as those of children and adults; neither can ever cross the boundary into the other's world. And that is the tragedy, and the pathos, of a poor man's life; the one that can help him cannot enter his world, and the one that can enter his world cannot help him. "Poor and proud," said the Master of Pen y Bryn and his wife; or at least, they hinted it on their way home, without saying it in so many words. It is true that pride — this sort of pride — has always been attracted to poverty throughout the ages, and every time they have married the union has been harmonious. True pride and honest poverty suit each other well.

The Pen y Bryn couple set off for home, their hearts bleeding for the poor, lonely little family, tucked away in that remote corner; the world was far, far away from them, yet tragedy had found its way to them. And they were surprised, and pitying, to find Sarah Ann Thomas acting in such a self-sufficient manner. Their conversation ran along these lines; but in the silences the Master of Pen y Bryn recalled that the last names on the lips of Mathew Thomas had been those of his wife and children. He understood them; and possibly the people he mentioned last were the only ones he had ever understood. Yes: Mathew Thomas understood his wife, and children, and Jesus, and he smiled when he died — when he *died.* His wife's behaviour, therefore, could not be too unworthy, or out of place in her husband's eyes — even if it cast a shadow on the infinite mercy of the Master of Pen y Bryn.

It was Christmas morning, and everyone's heart rejoiced to recall the babe born in Bethlehem; but it was not above the manger that the Master of Pen y Bryn spent the day, but above the bed of Mathew Thomas, watching him smiling as he lay dying, and facing the Great Nobleman in his Palace. He still had this mental conception of the place. He had heard many things about that land, but it was the last idea that stuck in his mind, just as the last look at a friend lingers in most people's minds. His thought had never dwelt on that place so much, in a short time, as it had done since the previous night. He had always had a nebulous sort of idea about it, somewhere in the remote corners of his soul. He, too, began to yearn for a glimpse of that territory, a glimpse from afar, before he had to face it himself — so that he could grow accustomed to the land. Sometimes he felt that he, the Master of Pen y Bryn, would be awarded greater honours there than a mere road-sweeper like Mathew Thomas. And yet, come to think of it, how little he knew about the place Mathew Thomas had gone to, on the threshold of which he had felt so much at ease. He had listened to sermons all his life, and he recited prayers publicly, but how little he had received from the gospel and from prayer! The gospel had lulled him into thinking that he was not as other men, and if he could get the saints to shout "Amen" when he prayed, he was well pleased with his prayer. For the saints, for him, were those who listened to him praying.

Often he had heard the hymn:
"Byth ni threulia
Tynion dannau'r delyn aur."
("The taut strings of the golden harp will never wear away"). He had felt, in some vague way, that the saints lived in a nebulous world of harp strings. But Mathew Thomas could not play the harp or anything else; and he had smiled as he lay dying. He had not realised before how vast the creation is, and how mysterious the ways of God. According to his profession of faith up to now, they had both been as clear as that two and two make four.

After seeing that smile, the Master of Pen y Bryn indulged in a long, cumbersome and tortuous contemplation for days. The soul's journey towards the light is a tortuous, indirect one. He tried to explain the smile, and the world Mathew Thomas had gone to, but he could not force himself to look that world in the face. At the start of each meditation session he would say to himself: "How happy I have been this last six months!" Then he would ask himself whether, in fact, he had been as happy as all that. Did he not remember some indefinable, restless urge in his soul, as far back as he *could* remember? Was it not the awakening of that urge that impelled him into the tithe war? And was it not the reawakening of that urge, in spite of himself, that made him subservient to David Hughes, and not any real danger from the actual man? Whatever Annie had done to save him from his clutches, he still felt a secret uneasiness about his dependence on Annie, even, for the maintenance of his self-respect and his status.

In view of all this, he was afraid of raising his gaze towards the land where Mathew Thomas went so happily. He was overcome with awe, then he pulled himself together, saying: "Now, even my old workman is making a doormat of me." And he lifted his eyes in a form of defiance towards the eternal powers that oppressed him. In his defiance, he despised everyone and everything; he even despised Mathew Thomas' family. But the cloud passed, and he saw a woman who refused to renounce the sacrifice which alleviated her sorrow — the sacrifice that involved struggling to pay for her family's mourning. He saw a small boy leaning on the mantelpiece in his nightshirt, with an ounce of tobacco for his father in his hand. When all was said and done, this was the only place where Mathew Thomas felt at home — with this woman, and these children; and he smiled as he lay dying. And this place he went to — was it, perhaps, not so much a nobleman's palace as a poor man's cottage; not Pen y Bryn but Y Pant? He had always thought that the being he called the Great Presence belonged to noble stock, as he did himself, but Mathew Thomas was smiling as he went to meet him. The problem weighed on him like lead, till all his petty worries became pleasures in his eyes, and music to his ears, compared with this one. He was so overwrought that he was determined to see this Lord that Mathew Thomas approached smiling, or die in the attempt. And it was in the solitude of night, early in the year, that he began his journey alone.

But it was a longer and harder journey than he had anticipated. He saw, everywhere on his path, the thorns and brambles of prejudice and dogma, convention and custom; and he tore himself apart as he ploughed his way through them. But the burden of creation, and the Great Beyond, and Mathew Thomas' smile, and every other mystery, were so overwhelming that he would have taken refuge among the thorns and the thickets, had he thought that these problems would not pursue him thither. He struggled onwards, with them in pursuit, till he came to the palace door of that mysterious Being he had been calling to all his life, without ever getting to know Him. He promised, in the madness of fervour, all the worldy goods he possessed. He pledged his status in the neighbourhood and his family traditions. He pleaded till the door opened and the Lord himself came into view, but the look He gave him was a strange one. He saw that He did not know the Master of Pen y Bryn; He had never heard his name; He had only heard of John Williams, and he could see from his face that He regarded John Williams as a poor and miserable sinner. After seeing that face, the problem of how Mathew Thomas could face this terrible Presence, and smile, became even more agonizing. He had heard, in the past, that this Being was Love, and he drew comfort from that. He saw now that He was, indeed, Love, but none the less terrible for that; for he discovered, when the battle was at its height, that love cannot love the unworthy.

Chapter XVI

Yes, John Williams discovered, in the heat of battle, that Love cannot love the unworthy, but he discovered, too, that Love has a greater glory than loving the unworthy; another kind of glory. This was the vision that came to him: that it cannot love the unworthy and the repugnant without self-betrayal, for it is its natural right to be proud of the object of its love. The glory of Love is not love of the unworthy, but the creation of an intercessor. It creates an intercessor in every heart it dwells in. It is Love that creates him, and Love that demands him. Love without an intercessor in its heart is not love at all. And everywhere it goes, it takes its intercessor with it. This is what John Williams discovered in the ferment of his soul.

The youth does not love the girl he has decided to share life with; she does not love him either. Rumour has it that he is unworthy of her, or *vice versa,* but they are still determined to spend life together, despite all the gossip. The lad does not love the girl who stands before him, but the image of her that he carries in his heart — an image created by his love of the only girl towards whom that love could flow. It is that image that he loves; his love created it and his love evoked it; he cannot be satisfied with anything less. It is in the heat of his passion for the image in his heart that he unites himself with the girl that incorporate that image, at some point, in her own being. His love for that image becomes a force which can elevate her to the status of the image. That image which his love created for itself is her intercessor before him. It is the same with the girl. She does not love the young man who stands before her, but the image of him which she dreams of; the image of a handsome youth, upright and faultless, and it is in her longing for that image to become flesh that she joins herself to the man. Each of their loves must have an intercessor, and the glory of love between a young man and a girl is its ability to create one.

A mother never loves the child who has fallen by the wayside. He is unworthy of love. It is not for his sake that she wasted away, and worried, and sacrificed, but for the sake of a beautiful image of a child which she carries in her heart. This was the one that captivated her before she ever set eyes on the other, and it is he who inspires her to suffer pain and want for his sake. And he is the product of her love, born of her desire for an object to delight in. Her love for him becomes an ennobling force to raise the real child from its degradation. And even when the child is on his feet, the image of him which makes him, for her, the best child in the world, is the pure creation of her love. The glory of a mother's love, too, is its creation of an intercessor.

As for the child himself: the ordinary woman who is his mother would not be the best woman in the world unless his love for her had created, for him, an image of the best mother in the world — and that image had acted as an intercessor for the ordinary woman.

A man laughs when he sees a sow wallowing in the mud, but he does not laugh when he sees his own sister doing the same thing. He does not have another image of the four-legged animal apart from the one he is confronted with. But because he is his sister's brother, he cherishes in his heart a sister without flaw or wrinkle, without bruise or deformity, without dirt or defilement. And it is that sister, the creation of his love, who extends a helping hand to the fallen sister, to show him that she, ennobled by the force of his love for the ideal sister, can raise the other up, and unite her with herself. The glory of a brother's love, like every other, is that it is a creator of intercessors.

John Williams found himself face to face with the Immortal Love, the Love that can only cherish the holy and the pure and the exalted; the Love whose heat scorched him and whose light blinded him. The eyes of the Immortal Love were fixed on some object beyond him and above him and around him, something he could not begin to grasp. And the smile which appeared on the face of the Immortal Love, as it gazed upon that object, was an awe-inspiring one. Then, slowly, it turned its gaze upon him, too, and away from that other object, just as the sun sinks towards the horizon. There was an incredible compassion and heartrending sorrow in that extraordinary gaze, when it met his own eyes; it turned everything he had ever gathered about him to ashes, leaving him naked and pitiful and lonely, terribly lonely, and forced to accept that compassionate gaze. From him, the gaze transferred itself back to the strange object which was beyond him, and above him, and around him. The gaze was so hypnotic that he could not help but follow it, though he sensed that it was presumptuous of him, in his sackcloth and ashes, to dare follow the gaze of the Immortal Love. He followed it till it fixed itself again on the strange object; and the man who had been degraded was astonished to see another John Williams standing beside him, protecting him with his shadow, someone just like himself, except that he was 'white and ruddy, the chiefest among ten thousand.' That John Williams was the creation of the Immortal Love, its own pride and joy. It was John Williams as depicted by that Love in its own heart, before his birth, as a mother creates the image of her child that she has never seen. And that John Williams had another name among men: the name Mathew Thomas Y Pant uttered, among the names of his dear ones, just before he died.

When he saw him, the degraded John Williams despised himself, and glorified himself at the same time. He saw how remote from him he was, but he saw, too, the greatness that he expected of him. And a deep, passionate, agonized yearning seized him, the desire for harmony with Him who resembled him so much, and yet was so remote from him. The sight of

Him made him cry out with hopelessness. He forgot every other trouble and torment in the pain which it gave his soul to drink in His beauty. He longed to be like Him, not because he feared a greater punishment from that compassionate soul whose suffering he could sense, but because He was so fair, and his beauty so hypnotic. He was the one who was the pride and joy of the Immortal Love. He was the image created by the great Love of the degraded John Williams, for he was his Father too. It was this image that led the Immortal Love to wait for him throughout the years, and to follow him through all the mud and the slime.

The image was so glorious that he could see that each man could give it a name of his own, without exhausting its virtues. It was the Immortal Love's creation of him, because it was a creation which sheltered mankind.

John Williams felt the magic of the Lord stealing over him — the Lord who entranced the Immortal Love, even. He stretched out his arms to Him, madly, so great was his craving for salvation, salvation from himself — because he could not bear that beauty any more without possessing it, without being consumed by it. And as he was stretching out his arms for very life, he felt something gripping him and pulling him to his feet. It was the Immortal Love, delighting in the Intercessor He had created — and this delight was creating in John Williams' soul the ability to incorporate The Intercessor within himself. This was happening because both of them, he and his Intercessor, were both children of the same Father. It was this that gripped him and drew him to his feet.

When he had risen, he looked around him like someone waking from a dream, and he found that he was in a new world, although it was night. He had been to the Nobleman's Palace, the one he called by a strange name, the Great Presence, but when he got there he discovered he was in his Father's house. He saw that up to now he had just been wandering haphazardly in one of the rooms, without getting to know the Master of the House; so he had mistaken his home for a prison. And from his Father's home John Williams saw that he could have the whole world as a footstool.

This was the experience John Williams won in the agony of his soul, and it was in these figures of speech, clumsily, that he tried to explain it to himself, or to anyone who showed him any sympathy. And this is the experience which is hidden from intellectuals and sophisticated people and revealed to little children.

Chapter XVII

There is no one like the Welshman for celebrating. To him a celebratory meeting ranks equal to the other main meetings in his calender, — a preaching festival, an eisteddfod, a funeral.

One Sunday morning in January, after the service, the Rev. T. Cefnllech Roberts called the officials of Bethania together to decide whether it would be appropriate to hold a special fellowship meeting, in honour of those heroic members of the chapel who had been courageous enough, the year before, to stand by their principles and oppose authority — by not paying the tithe. Then, perhaps, they could have a celebration meeting for the whole neighbourhood later. It was just a year, he said, since the auctions began, and the occasion should not pass unnoticed, for the sake of the young people. Was it not on them that the future of Wales depended — Wales, that was so ready to awaken and face the dawn? The heroes opposed the suggestion. John Williams remembered a certain very recent evening in his life, and looked uneasy. But their modest attitude was very easy to understand, said the minister, and it was decided to hold a special fellowship meeting, by way of celebration, within the week.

The chapel was overflowing on the night. The minister presided, and he asked John Owen the cobbler, Bethania's most gifted practitioner of spontaneous public prayer, to start the meeting going. John Owen asked the Almighty to open the heart of the Old Mother Church. Her children had left her because she had turned nasty on them, but really they thought the world of her, for she was their mother, after all. And the burden of every entreaty was: "Bestow Thy grace on the Old Mother Church, great Lord, and open her eyes; she is going blind, thou canst be sure." He assured the Almighty that there were no hard feelings between them and Old Mother Church, that it was all her fault, and that they were all ready to fly back into her arms when He had bestowed His grace upon her and opened her eyes. Having assured the Lord of this, he asked for His blessing upon the meeting. "No doubt, Lord," he said, "the heroes will feel a bit shy of praising themselves but give us the grace to praise them with ready tongue." This was a good start to the meeting.

The minister spoke first. He stressed how Wales was awakening, and with a few variations on his perpetual theme he described how the dawn was rising on Wales, shackles were being cast aside, the yoke of centuries of oppression was being removed, the mountains were shouting and singing, the trees were applauding, and so forth. He urged the young people of Wales to carry the banner onwards till they reached the crest of the hill of victory, and then plant it for ever there. He knew, he said, that not everyone in that church was of the same opinion as the heroes — that one should not pay the tithe — but that everyone was entitled to his opinion, and no one bore a grudge against them, he was sure, because they thought differently. He assured them that the glory of religion was that it respected every man who was true to his principles. David Hughes, the carpenter, was present.

When the minister had finished, he called on a few minor speakers to say a few words, to get them out of the way. He had arranged the programme competently, keeping John Williams till the end, because he knew he was an effective speaker and because it was his heroism that had fired public imagination the most.

After the minor speakers, the Master of Y Bryniau was called, and he spoke wisely, praising everyone except himself. After him Samuel Jones, Y Tŷ Glas was called upon. Samuel

Jones could not understand, he said, why such a meeting was necessary; he had only done his duty according to his lights as, indeed, he tried to do every single day, but he didn't want a celebration meeting in honour of every day of his life. The minister and every other supporter dutifully said "hear, hear," during this speech, intimating that they understood this attitude very well and that it was a worthy one.

When Samuel Jones had sat down, someone struck up a hymn, to try and create a sort of revivalist atmosphere. Then the minister called on two or three other people, and eventually the turn of John Williams, Pen y Bryn, came. He called on him to give the young people a word of advice about the best way to face life's battles.

He got up very slowly, and the "hear, hears" started up before he had commenced to speak — to help him, probably. Verbal supporters, too, are merciful beings — sometimes. He got up hesitantly, and wound his arm round the lamp post at the corner of his pew. His spouse sat next to him; she had been overwhelmed by strong emotions for quite a time.

"Brothers and sisters," he said, then he was silent for a moment, as if he was trying to contain the conflict in his breast. The minister and one or two of the others "hear heared" him as much as ever. "Brothers and sisters," he said again, and stood there, swallowing a lump in his throat that insisted on rising in spite of him. "Hear hear, God be praised, hear hear," said the minister and the other supporters. But this did not seem to be helping John Williams very much; and he was usually greatly influenced by verbal support.

"Well," he said, when he was able to control himself a little, "this is what I've been thinking. We are taught, every day, that we are travellers on a journey, just as the river makes its journey to the sea," and he was silent for a moment again to contain the conflict, and the supporters' "hear hear," and "thanks be to God" rose rapidly like a tide. He started again: "The river is journeying on; but in spite of this, when the weather is cold we can see it cleaving to the earth. It is the same with us." He was silent another moment, and the support was vociferous and enthusiastic. It was obvious that John Williams was all set for the "hwyl".

"Friends," he said presently, "I am an old river which has clung a great deal to the earth — the earth of other people's opinion, the earth of possessions, the earth of selfishness, and being on good terms with myself — these were the fruits of that earth," and he was silent again. "No, no, thanks be to God, no, not at all," said the supporters, many of them in tears by this time. "But the river is beginning to slacken its grip on the earth," he said. "Thanks be to God, hear hear," said the minister, echoed now by a multitude of supporters.

"There was a lot of sheep killing at the beginning of last summer," said John Williams, and everyone fell silent, uncertain what to expect. "One of the dogs was Shep Y Foty," he said, "and our Rover killed him," and a few people started to sing Rover's praises. "Yes, and the other dog was Rover. I kept it to myself for a long time, because I was afraid people would despise me, but I see now that there is no disgrace in being honest, whatever the cost." By now the whole place was silent as the grave, and John Williams went on.

"Many people have suffered through being heroes of the tithe war," he said, "but I haven't suffered at all — outwardly. Do you know why? Because I fell on my knees like a contemptible piece of rag in front of the bishop, to ask his pardon. This is the kind of hero I was. You will despise me, and I deserve it, but be that as it may, the contempt of one's countrymen is preferable to a dishonest heart. Samuel Jones here is a hero, and the Master of Y Bryniau too, and the others from other denominations are heroes, but I refused to pay the tithe only because I was afraid of people. But what is the fear of people compared with the fear of God?"

He almost betrayed the secret of his great conflict, but he remembered that the paths he trod to his Father's house were thorny ones, and he did not want to reveal that Home to anyone who was unwilling to tread those paths. He was silent a moment, to collect his thoughts. "The river has begun to thaw now," he said; "yes, it has." He was still standing with his arm around the lamp post at the corner of his pew, gazing at some point above the congregation, without saying a word; his face was quiet, restful and serene.

When he had stopped speaking everyone looked at each other and at him in turn; the minister hung his head, looking like a man overcome by failure; for his sun, like everyone else's, had set, while it was still daylight. It remained that way for a moment, with everyone expecting someone else to act. The minister rose suddenly, and raised his hand over the congregation. "Let us end," he said.

"ThegraceofourLordJesusChristandtheloveofGodandthe FellowshipoftheHolyGhostbewithusallAmen,"

and he sat down. Silence again for a moment. A few people began to shuffle around, the congregation arose like one man, and they went out. The minister got up too, and followed the others out, through the door which was furthest away from John Williams; and John Williams was still standing in the same place, looking quietly, calmly and serenely at the departing congregation, as if he were completely detached from it. Everyone walked out in silent batches at first, then the tongues began to wag. Margaret Jones, Y Ty Glas, was the most voluble, though it was a kind of whisper; she sounded very pleased with herself. The minister followed the congregation, a disappointed man.

But John Williams was not left alone. One man sat down when everyone else had gone: Samuel Jones, Y Tŷ Glas. David Hughes, the carpenter, got up with the rest, made for the door, stood still, hesitated, and sat down. When they had all disappeared Samuel Jones walked over to John Williams. The latter gazed at him, smiling uneasily. He was not very sure of this man who did not know what it meant to be a hero, who knew of nothing except duty. Samuel Jones had a rugged face, like a crag, but as he approached John Williams it softened like the face of a crag in the summer sun. He offered him his hand, and said in a voice which was, for him, incredibly tender and gentle: "John Williams, I never knew the meaning of heroism till tonight. My old heart is lonely and ignorant, and it wants to learn; may I be your friend?" John Williams gave him his hand and looked deep into his eyes and his lips trembled.

David Hughes approached them, slowly and hesitantly. "John Williams," he said, less self-controlled than he had ever been before, "will you lead me, too, into this new life? I don't understand it properly, but I feel certain that I'm face to face with something great." He, too, extended his hand, and they squeezed each other's hands for a long time.

The minister was in a very bitter mood after the failure of the meeting, and he walked home alone to give full rein to his bitterness. "How can Wales awaken properly," he said, "with such men living here? He may have asked the bishop for forgiveness, but what good does it do to admit that to people who scorn all heroism?" His mind was running on this tack as he went along the footpath towards the house. He remembered the celebration concert, and his efforts to get the Master of Pen y Bryn as chairman; all that effort was wasted now. The Master of Pen y Bryn, and everything connected with him, would always be a laughing stock after this. He recalled the night John Williams and his wife came to ask him to clear the way for him to be chairman; he remembered his own promise, and how he had stood for a long time in the hall at home, after selling his soul tohim and saying good night. The thoughts that had raced through his mind on that occasion raced through his mind again. He stood and clapped his hands to his forehead, as if a lightning flash had illuminated his path in the dark. He stayed like that for a while, then turned back, slowly and uncertainly; but as he proceeded his pace quickened, till it became a half-trot when he saw a light in the chapel.

He went into the porch and looked furtively round the edge of the door, and saw John Williams standing with his arm round the lamp post, with the other two men standing before him. All three faces shone with a transforming light. He opened the door and went to them, walking very shakily. He grasped John Williams' hand with both of his, and said quietly, and inarticulately, and nervously, like a man who has just seen an apparition, "John Williams, my visions are being resurrected, one after another; and each one of them is full of the might of the resurrection — each one! That is something which came from you. There was no hope of their resurrection through anything in me." John Williams did not know what he was referring to, but he understood well enough, and everyone started off home, and they all understood.

As he walked alone up the hill towards home, John Williams raised his eyes upwards. How honest, and unequivocal, and friendly the stars looked as they gazed down at him; they had always been so strange before. He went on to the grove near the house, and as he approached he felt it was encircling him like the arms of a mother encircling her child; and each tree looked so honest, and unequivocal, and friendly, though they had looked so strangely and blankly at him for so long. He could not remember seeing them look like this, ever since he played among them as a small child. When he had passed through the grove he looked around him, and there was a kind of honesty and uprightness and friendliness everywhere on the face of the earth, and he felt it would not be unpleasant to lie in her bosom at his journey's end, with the earth tightening her arms around him and clasping him to her breast. These were the thoughts that came to John Williams, Pen y Bryn, as he achieved a feeling of harmony with the Source of all Being. The lesson he learned in the fellowship of the Immortal Love was that the creation had been founded on homely virtues, after all; otherwise, a man like Mathew Thomas, Y Pant, of all people, would never have smiled as he died.

When he got to the house, his wife was sitting by the fire, crying, and Lizzie was comforting her. Annie, who was getting supper ready, gazed at him as if she were gazing at the invisible; but there was a light in her eyes which does not shine except through the eyes of the soul, and in the great moments of existence. His wife turned to him and looked at him through her tears, her gaze full of woe. Yes, her idols had all been shattered to pieces, and all she had lived and schemed for was lost. Yet through it all another look shone, like the look on the face of a child at the seaside when he gazes at the great depths. The ocean is so great that it mystifies him, but its greatness entrances him so much that he simply cannot leave its shores to play with his own little puddle, though that may be nearer to his own world. As time passed, Jane Williams' look of disappointment faded, and her expression grew more like that of the child at the seaside. And the longer she stood on the shore, the more she was captivated by the magic of the sea. And Jane Williams, for the rest of her life, was ensnared by the magic of a sea she did not understand.

Chapter XVIII

The years came and went, and brought many changes; and Annie became the Mistress of Pen y Bryn. The little pony had returned to its old haunts, and the girl that once loved it so much had the pleasure of seeing some of her own children riding it.

One evening, on a pleasant summer's day, the Mistress of Pen y Bryn heard footsteps coming up the yard, and she got to the door in time to see Rover, who was old and blind now, slipping out of sight round the corner of the barn like a youngster.

"Hello, David Hughes," she said, when she saw the man, on whom age was beginning to leave its mark, coming to the door, "how are you tonight?"

"Quite well, thanks, Annie my dear," said David Hughes, "how's the old man — and the family?"

"We're fine, thanks," said Annie, "but my father — he's not well at all. He's getting very forgetful, and talks to himself a lot, and goes on about mother all the time. Come inside, do; I'll call him. You'll cheer him up a lot."

"When did you hear from Lizzie? She hasn't been home for some time," said David Hughes.

"This morning," said Annie. "She's fine, and talking about coming home before the end of summer. Where's dad, I wonder?" She looked outside and shouted "D-aad," but no one answered.

Shôn Bach poked his head out from the cowshed. "Shôn,"

said Annie, "have you seen my father anywhere? David Hughes is here."

"He was passing this door just now," said Shôn, and went on with his work. He was still Little Shôn, though he had been chief labourer at Pen y Bryn for years, and had set up house with Mary Eliza.

"Never mind," said David Hughes, "he'll show up eventually. Somehow I couldn't feel comfortable at home this fine night, without much to do; so I thought I'd come for a chat."

"And quite right too," said Annie.

She went to the door again, and shouted "Da-ad," once more till the place re-echoed, but her father was out of earshot.

The pair of them chatted for a while, and the master of the house entered — formerly the son from Plas Isaf. "Have you seen dad around?" Annie asked him as soon as he set foot on the threshold.

"I saw him about half an hour ago — he looked as if he was going for a walk," he replied; "he went towards the barn," and he sat down to talk to David Hughes.

But John Williams did not come back, though they waited a long time for him. Annie went to the door again, and saw Rover standing at the barn door looking as if he were enjoying the scene before him in a solemn, melancholy way, an appropriate way for an old, blind dog to enjoy the scenery. "Rover is at the barn door, large as life," she said: "I wonder if dad is in there?"

"I'll go and see," said David Hughes. "I may as well chat to him in there as anywhere else on a fine night like this," and off he went. As soon as he set foot in the yard Rover turned tail and disappeared into the barn, and he, too, made his way there.

When he got there he found John Williams sitting on a block of wood before an old round table, his head resting on his arms, his eyes closed in sleep, and a calm smile on his face; Rover was hanging his head and nestling between his legs for all he was worth.

"Hello," said David Hughes loudly. "It's very close today, and we're not getting any younger, are we?" But John Williams did not move, and he did not open his eyes. David Hughes hastened towards him, and saw at once that those eyes would never open again. John Williams held a pencil stump in his hand, and there was a piece of paper on the floor at his feet. David Hughes picked up the paper; on it, in a clumsy hand, were the words:

Jane died 1889
Our wedding 1863
26 yea

and the "yea" tailed off into a shaky scribble and into nothingness.

David Hughes looked at the paper, and from it he gazed, through a mist, at John Williams. He seemed to be sleeping so peacefully, and his smile was so charming, that it seemed a pity to touch him, lest his own illusion — that he was sleeping — should be shattered.

He looked at Rover, and caressed him lovingly again and again.

"Rover, old boy," he said, "now you're all alone too, aren't you? But never mind, Rover old boy, you'll find a friend somewhere."

David Hughes went to the house, without touching the man who sat at the table, smiling peacefully in his sleep. Rover followed him like a bosom friend. And when, in due course, he set off for home, having done his best to calm the fury of this sudden tempest, Rover insisted on following him, and follow him he did.